*"I'm not making visits to the Silver Horn ranch for your amusement, Mr. Calhoun."*

"How could anything so cold come out of such a beautiful mouth?" he countered. "Especially when I haven't given you a reason to dislike me."

She breathed deeply and assured herself that she wasn't feeling an ounce of attraction for this man. "I've not given you any reason to flirt with me either," she said stiffly.

Instead of making him angry, her response merely made him laugh. Again. And Lilly was shocked at how the low, rich sound sent a shiver of pleasure right through her.

"You're definitely a saucy little thing."

And he was just the sort of man that Lilly had taken great pains to avoid these past few years. "I'm not a thing, Mr. Calhoun. I'm a woman."

The corner of his lips curved upward. "Yes, I can see exactly how much of a woman."

* * *

**Men of the West:**
**Whether ranchers or lawmen,**
**these heartbreakers can ride, shoot**
**and drive a woman crazy....**

Dear Reader,

Welcome back to the Silver Horn! It's springtime and round-up on the massive ranch is in full swing. At the center of all the hubbub is the foreman, Rafe, the middle of the five Calhoun brothers. He's one hunk of a rugged cowboy, who spends his days in the saddle and his nights enjoying the ladies. His father, Orin, has called Rafe the spirit of the ranch, and nothing could be more true. He's dead serious about keeping the heart of the ranch beating strongly, but as for his own heart, he keeps it safely tucked away behind a charming grin and lines of smooth talk.

When I first met the Calhoun family, I expected Rafe to be the last of the brothers to succumb to love. After all, his determination to stay single is as tough as a rawhide quirt. And flitting from one woman to the next is as natural for him as a honeybee tasting every flower in the garden. But then a strong-willed nurse comes to the ranch and she seems to have the perfect prescription to change his bachelor ways.

Rafe's journey to love took me on an emotional roller coaster...and for a while I feared that even Lilly wasn't up to the task of taming her cowboy. But love has a way of taking control, no matter how hard the fight.

I hope you enjoy Rafe's story and please stay tuned to see what happens next on the Silver Horn Ranch.

God bless each trail you ride,

Stella Bagwell

# One Tall, Dusty Cowboy

—

## Stella Bagwell

HARLEQUIN® SPECIAL EDITION®

Recycling programs
for this product may
not exist in your area.

ISBN-13: 978-0-373-65831-2

ONE TALL, DUSTY COWBOY

Printed in U.S.A.

## *STELLA BAGWELL*

has written more than seventy novels for Harlequin. She credits her loyal readers and hopes her stories have brightened their lives in some small way. A cowgirl through and through, she loves to watch old Westerns, and has recently learned how to rope a steer. Her days begin and end helping her husband care for a beloved herd of horses on their little ranch located on the south Texas coast. When she's not ropin' and ridin', you'll find her at her desk, creating her next tale of love. The couple has a son, who is a high school math teacher and athletic coach. Stella loves to hear from readers and invites them to contact her at stellabagwell@gmail.com.

To my late brother-in-law, Gerald Foster, and
the loving memories I will always carry in my heart.

## Chapter One

The man standing at the foot of the long staircase was one tall, dusty cowboy and looked entirely out of place standing on the polished wood floor in his boots and spurs and bat-wing chaps. A straw hat was pulled low over his forehead, but the moment he spotted her descending the long steps, he swept it off to reveal thick waves of varying shades of chestnut. Yet it was the speculative gaze on his face that jarred Lilly Lockett the most and prompted her to lift her chin to a challenging tilt.

She halted two steps from where he stood with a gloved hand resting on the polished balustrade. "Are you lost?"

To her dismay, he threw back his head and howled with laughter. "A few folks around here would say I'm lost all the time, Ms...?"

The unsettling glint in his eyes put a prim note to her voice. "Lilly Lockett. And you are?"

Climbing one step closer, he jerked off a scarred leather glove and extended his hand to her. "Rafe Calhoun, at your service, ma'am."

Lilly wasn't sure if the blush warming her face was because the man was touching her or because she'd mistaken a member of the Calhoun family for a common ranch hand.

"Hello, Rafe Calhoun. Are you Bart's son or grandson?"

His outlandish grin was bracketed by a pair of incredible dimples, but they only made up a small part of this man's striking looks. His skin was tanned to a deep nut-brown, making a pair of gray eyes stand out beneath hooded brows. Chiseled cheekbones angled downward to a proud, hawkish nose and lean cheeks, while a hank of rusty-brown hair flopped onto a high forehead. She'd heard through the rumor mill that one of the Calhoun boys was a player with the ladies and from the looks of this one she'd pretty much bet him to be the culprit.

"Bart is my grandfather." His gaze slipped from her face to her bare ring finger then farther downward over her navy blue scrubs. "Are you here to treat him?"

Determined not to allow this rakish cowboy to rattle her senses for one moment longer, she pulled her hand from his and stiffened her already straight spine. "I'm Mr. Calhoun's—Bart's physical therapist. I'll be working with him the next few weeks."

If possible, the grin on Rafe Calhoun's face grew even deeper. "Well, now, that's the best news I've heard in days."

Her back teeth clamped together. "Really? The fact that your grandfather has had a stroke and needs physical therapy is good news to you?"

"Aw, now, Lilly," he began in a slow, flirtatious drawl. "That wasn't even close to what I meant."

Not about to give this man an opportunity to work his charms on her, she said, "It was nice to meet you, Mr. Calhoun. Now if you'll excuse me, I have to be at the hospital in forty-five minutes."

He stroked a thoughtful finger along his jaw. "It only takes thirty minutes to get to town from here. Surely you can give me five of those extra ones."

"What makes you think you deserve five minutes of my time?"

The question appeared to take him aback and while he was searching for words, she stepped around him and started across a wide corridor that would eventually lead her to a side exit of the huge ranch house. Rafe Calhoun's jingle-bell spurs rang out as he hurried after her.

"Now wait a minute, Lilly. You're not being very friendly. You don't want to give me a bad first impression, do you?"

Pausing, she turned to find him standing directly behind her and so close that she could smell the dust and sweat on his clothes, see the gray horse hair and streaks of dirt clinging to his white shirt. Now that the grin had been wiped from his face, she was able to observe his lips in their natural state. They were thin and hard with a tiny white scar adorning the top corner. Apparently, at one time, something or someone had busted his mouth.

The man probably liked fighting as much as he liked kissing, she couldn't help thinking.

"I'm not interested in giving you any sort of impression. I'm not making visits to the Silver Horn ranch for your amusement, Mr. Calhoun. I'm here to treat your grandfather. Now goodbye!"

"How could anything so cold come out of such a beautiful mouth?" he countered. "Especially when I haven't given you a reason to dislike me."

She breathed deeply and assured herself that she wasn't feeling an ounce of attraction for this man. She was simply fascinated by his rough, tough appearance and the easy way all those pretty words rolled from his tongue.

"I've not given you any reason to flirt with me, either," she said stiffly.

Instead of making him angry, her response merely made him laugh. Again. And Lilly was shocked at how the low, rich sound sent a shiver of pleasure right through her.

"You're definitely a saucy little thing."

And he was just the sort of man that Lilly had taken great pains to avoid these past few years. "I'm not a thing, Mr. Calhoun. I'm a woman."

The corner of his lips, the one with the fetching little scar, curved upward. "Yes, I can see exactly how much of a woman."

Incensed, she said, "If that's the case, then go find the nearest mirror and tell the guy looking back at you that he's not quite the Romeo he thinks he is."

With that she didn't wait around for his response. Instead, she walked quickly away from him until she was completely outside of the house. Fifteen minutes later, she'd driven halfway to Carson City and by then she realized her fingers were aching from the choke hold she had on the steering wheel.

What was she doing? Why had she let a playboy's silly flirtation get her riled? At twenty-eight years of age and working most of her adult life as a nurse, she'd dealt with all types of men. And she understood that the majority of them had one thing on their minds. It was obvious that Rafe Calhoun was no different.

Shoving a hand through her shoulder-length blond hair, she kept her eyes on the highway while she fought to push the man's image from her mind. She hoped to heaven she wouldn't run into him again, but she seriously doubted she could be that lucky. She'd only started Bart Calhoun's therapy three days ago and the task of rehabilitating the use of his leg and arm was going to be long and arduous. And given Rafe Calhoun's persistence, she had the sinking feeling he would make it a point to bump into her whenever she was at the ranch.

*You can't be worrying about that, Lilly. Men like him are everywhere. And for the past seven years you've managed very well to stay out of their reach. You can stay out of Rafe's path, too.*

But that was going to be easier said than done, she thought, as she pulled into a parking space set aside for hospital personnel. Men like Rafe weren't exactly everywhere. There had been something about him that had struck a nerve and made her so totally aware of the long months she'd gone without so much as having a man hold her hand. And that sad fact was hardly something she wanted to dwell on.

"Good morning, Lilly. How did it go with Mr. Calhoun this morning?"

As Lilly passed the nurses' station, she glanced over to see Jolene, a young brunette nurse that worked the morning shift in the E.R.

"He's trying his best."

"Well, I'd sure like a job inside that fancy mansion, but I wouldn't want to deal with Mr. Calhoun. I've heard stories about his last visit here at the hospital. He had most of the nurses in tears or wanting to kill him." Gesturing over her shoulder in the direction of the snack room, she said, "I saved you a couple of pieces of pizza for lunch. It's in the fridge if you want it."

"Thanks, Jolene. Maybe later. Right now I'm running short on time."

Thanks to one sexy cowboy with a glib tongue. She wondered what Jolene or any of the other nurses could tell her about Rafe Calhoun. Probably the same thing that was said about the elder Calhoun, she thought; he left women in tears or wanting to kill him.

Back on the Silver Horn, Rafe stepped into his father's office and walked straight to the coffeepot.

"What's up? I thought branding was going on today?" Orin asked.

Rafe glanced over at the big man sitting behind a wide mahogany desk. In his early sixties, Orin Calhoun was still as strong and vital as he'd been twenty years ago. The only difference now was that his hair was more gray than dark and age lines creased the corners of his eyes and mouth. Orin had raised five strapping sons and along the way lost the only woman he'd ever loved. Rafe seriously doubted he could ever be as great a man as his father, so most of the time he didn't try.

"Branding is going on," Rafe answered. "I burnt the hell out of my finger and had to come get another pair of gloves."

Orin frowned. "We keep stacks of gloves in every barn."

"Well, I had to put some ointment on my finger and I wanted my own gloves. Come to think of it, I should've let that pretty little nurse of Gramps's treat me. Bet she would've known exactly what to do to take out the sting."

As Rafe sipped the black coffee, he watched his father let out a weary sigh. It was no secret that Orin didn't like Rafe's philandering ways. He'd often hounded Rafe to either settle down with a woman or, at the very least, quit chasing them like a bull in a spring pasture full of heifers. But Rafe was thirty years old and though he was open to advice, he lived life his own way and at his own pace.

"Son, I hope I don't have to tell you to behave like a gentleman around Ms. Lockett. She's a specialist in therapy, but also works in the E.R. at Tahoe General. She's only taken this job as a favor to Chet Anderson, the director of nursing there, who also happens to be a friend of mine. And it would be damned hard to replace her," he added with a pointed glance at Rafe.

Walking over to the wide window overlooking the ranch yard, Rafe gazed over the rim of his coffee cup at the busy comings and goings of the hired hands. Except for a two-year stint in college, he'd spent his entire life on this Nevada ranch. Five years ago, his grandfather, Bart, had appointed him the position of ranch foreman and during those five years Rafe wasn't sure if Bart had cursed or blessed him. Overseeing twenty-five men, thousands of head of cattle and several sections of rugged ranch land had never been a simple task. In the very beginning Rafe had stumbled more than once, and there had been times he'd even doubted his ability to handle a job that normally would go to a much older, more experienced man. But he'd been determined to prove his worth and now being the foreman of the Silver Horn was a job he lived, slept and breathed.

"What's the matter with you, Dad?"

Orin let out another sigh and the sound irked Rafe no end. He loved and respected his father greatly, but it annoyed the hell out of Rafe to have the other man treat him as though he were still a bumbling teenager.

"All right, son. Just so you understand how important she is right now. She could be the difference in your grandfather getting strong enough to walk again."

Rafe turned away from the window. "You make it sound like she's a miracle worker."

"From what Chet told me, she has worked miracles with a few hopeless cases. That's why he recommended her for Dad's therapy. I just hope she can endure his bullheadedness."

From his brief exchange with the blonde beauty, he certainly didn't think she'd have any trouble holding her own with Bart. She was the first woman in a long time that had rejected his advances, and she'd hardly been uncertain about it.

*Go find the nearest mirror and tell the guy looking back at you that he's not quite the Romeo he thinks he is.*

Lilly Lockett's parting remark still had enough power to sting him. But on the other hand, he admired her spunk. And Rafe always did like a challenge.

"Don't worry, Dad. I don't think Lilly is the sort of woman who runs from anything. She'll handle Gramps." *And me,* he thought wryly.

"I'm glad you think so. Now tell me about the branding. Did the men find more stray calves to add to the spring tally?"

"Fifty-two additional head. They were over on the Antelope Range, on the flats near the river. All of them were packing good weight."

"That's a nice find. Have you tagged or branded them yet?"

"No, sir. I plan to start on them before the end of the week. We'll do the bunch over on the Salt Cedar trail first." Rafe quickly drained the last of his coffee then put the cup down on the coffee table. "I'd better get back out to the branding fire. I'll see you at supper."

As he started out of the office, his father called out, "Rafe? Did you come all the way upstairs just for a cup of coffee?"

Damn! Meeting Lilly Lockett on the staircase must have distracted him more than he thought. "Oh, yeah. I wanted to talk to you about those horses Finn has been lobbying for. Is he going to get them or not? The hands are hurting for more mounts. Three are sidelined with bone chips and two more are being treated for colic and one with a shoulder injury."

"Have you talked to Finn about this?"

Frustrated, Rafe slapped his gloves against the palm of his hand. "Hell, yes. He says he'll come up with more. But damn it, Dad, he's so caught up with the foaling mares he forgets that there's cattle to be taken care of around here. It's already the first week of May. We can't do the rest of spring roundup without horses."

"Have you talked with your brother today?"

"I went by the foaling barn but he wasn't there. I tried his cell phone but he didn't answer."

"He's probably over at the J Bar S. He promised Sassy he'd help her with one of their horses. I don't know exactly what it was about but you know how Finn feels about his sister. He's not about to disappoint her."

A little more than a year ago, it was revealed that Orin had sired a daughter during a brief, illicit affair. Not only had it shocked Orin, who'd been unaware of the child, it had stunned Rafe and his four brothers to learn they had a half-sister. But learning their father had been unfaithful to their mother had only been a part of the revelation. The whole secret of the woman's pregnancy had been kept for twenty-four years with hush money doled out by Bart.

No doubt the story had been told and retold from one end of Carson City to the other.

"I love Sassy, too," Rafe said. "But Finn needs to get his priorities straight! If he doesn't have time to take care of the working remuda, then maybe you ought to find someone who can!"

Rising to his feet, Orin leveled a look of warning at him. "Rafe! You're stepping out of line."

Rafe stood his ground. "Sorry, Dad, but I'm stepping exactly where I should be stepping. This whole matter reflects on my job and I'm not going to let anyone make me look like a slacker!"

With a weary shake of his head, Orin asked quietly, "Does this always have to come down to you, Rafe?"

"I'm thinking about this ranch. Not myself. Maybe someday you and everybody else around here will understand that."

He left the office before his father could say more and once outside, his long stride carried him toward a group of wooden corrals, where he'd left his horse tethered to a hitching rail. As he mounted the blue roan and kicked the gelding into a lope, he realized it was a waste of time to try to argue his case with his father. Neither Orin nor his brothers really understood what drove or pushed him. They all believed he was self-seeking. They had no clue that every cell of his heart had long ago been poured into this land and the animals that roamed it.

* * *

The next morning, Lilly was relieved when she entered the Silver Horn ranch house and made it up to Bart's room without running into Rafe. Not that she'd been expecting him to be lurking around, just waiting to see her again. But even the thought of a chance meeting with the man ruffled her nerves. Especially after the fourteen-hour shift she'd put in yesterday. One traumatic injury after another had come through the E.R. doors over the course of the night, and she'd finally crawled into bed just before daylight, mentally drained and physically exhausted.

"You're going to have to do better than that, Bart," she said a few minutes later as she urged the man to make another repetitive move with his arm. "Use all your strength. Keep your hand against mine and try to shove me backwards."

The white-haired man chuckled. "I'd never shove a lovely lady like you, Lilly."

Lilly couldn't help but smile. Everyone had warned her that Bart Calhoun was a hateful, crotchety bastard of a man, but from the moment she'd met him, he'd been a perfect gentleman. She only hoped his manners didn't change before his therapy was finished.

"Well, just pretend that I'm someone you don't like," she told him. "And don't worry, I'm strong. So put some power in that arm."

He did as she asked and this time she could feel a bit more resistance as he strained to do the exercise.

"I've never been helpless in my life, Lilly. And I don't like it. Up until I had the stroke, I still had enough punch to knock a man flat on his back. But now..." He trailed off with a wistful sigh. "Things change when a man gets older."

Moving to his left foot, she motioned for him to push against her cupped hands. "You can't blame your condition on your age, Bart. From what your family tells me, you like Kentucky bourbon and arguing. That's not a good combination for a man with high blood pressure."

"Well, I do have my faults," he sheepishly admitted. "All of us men do, you know. I'm just thankful to God that my speech wasn't affected. It would be hell if I couldn't communicate."

Lilly figured this man didn't necessarily need words to communicate. He was very much like his grandson, who expressed most of his thoughts through his eyes.

"Or heck if you couldn't argue," she teased as she continued to put his leg through a series of motions. "I hope your speech wasn't spared for that reason."

He didn't say anything and after a few moments she glanced up to see he was studying her with a thoughtful eye. "Are you married, Lilly?"

She cast him a coy glance. "No. Why? Do you have matrimony on your mind?"

He chuckled. "Well, you'd certainly tempt a man to stand in front of the preacher. But no. I've only loved one woman in my life and she died twenty years ago. I can't imagine myself with another wife."

His sentiment touched her more than he could ever know. Her parents had been married for nearly thirty years, yet she'd never seen much affection expressed between them. Certainly not the kind of love or devotion that Bart felt for his late wife. After all these years, Lilly wasn't sure what had kept her parents together. Her father, Ron Lockett, had always been a quiet, hardworking man who was content to live modestly. On the other hand, her mother, Faye, was never content and was always demanding her husband to change and follow her wants and wishes, which caused a constant clash of differences between the two.

As a child, her parents' dysfunctional marriage had affected Lilly deeply. By the time she'd entered her teen years, she'd sworn that her life was going to be different. She would love the man she married and he would love her equally. There wouldn't be arguing, threats or tears. But now, years later, she'd learned that love wasn't that easy to find and life had a way of producing tears.

"I've never been married," she told Bart.

"How come? You don't like men?"

She let out a silent sigh. "I like them. I just haven't found one I like enough to share the rest of my life with. I'm particular, I suppose."

"Particular is good. That means you're smart."

Smart? In many ways Lilly supposed she was smart. She had a good education and she'd been told by many of her peers that she was an excellent and intelligent nurse. But in her personal life, she'd made mistakes she was still trying to forget.

She glanced over at the large window and a view of the distant desert hills. The Silver Horn was known far and wide for its wealth, horses and cowboys. And though she wasn't familiar with ranch life, she had to admit this place, and the family who ran it, intrigued her.

"Did you live on this ranch when you got married?" she asked Bart.

"Yes. But it wasn't the place it is now. My father started the Horn back in 1909 from just a bare spot— where the barns are now. Over time as his herd multiplied, he bought more land. Eventually, his profit grew and he sank part of it in lucrative investments. That's how it all got started. By the time he died in 1960 I was in my thirties, so I took over and tried to follow in his footsteps."

"Well, your father clearly taught you well. It's a beautiful place," Lilly told him. "You must be very proud."

"I'm more proud of my grandsons," he said, then added, "When I get better I'm going to personally show you around the ranch. How would you like that, Lilly?"

Glancing around, she smiled at the elder Calhoun. "It's a date."

Bart chuckled and something about the smug sound reminded Lilly of Rafe. Like grandfather, like grandson? No. Bart had clearly loved his wife, whereas Rafe would never settle for one woman.

A half hour later Bart had completed his therapy for the day and Lilly was driving down the long drive that led away from the house, when a horse and rider suddenly galloped up beside the car.

Slightly panicked by the nearness of the animal to her vehicle door, she jammed on the brakes and the small car came to a jarring halt in the middle of the road.

By the time she'd collected herself enough to look around, Rafe had already leaped from the saddle and was standing next to the door, motioning for her to lower the window.

As soon as the glass was no longer a screen between them, she blasted, "Are you out of your mind? You could have killed both of us!"

Laughing at her discomfiture, he said, "Roscoe knew

what he was doing. He could thread through a stand of brush without ever getting a scratch."

His grinning face made her want to groan and laugh at the same time. "I'm glad your Roscoe knew what he was doing because you certainly didn't!"

"Since you don't really know me, I'm not going to take that comment to heart."

His gray eyes were gliding over her face like slow, searching fingers, touching each contour of each feature. And suddenly she was acutely aware of her bare face and the messy bun pinned atop her head. "You can take it any way you'd like, Mr. Calhoun. But I need to be on my way. Would you like to get to your reason for this dramatic stop?"

"I wanted to see you again. That's the reason."

Her nostrils flared. "I should have guessed it wasn't to inquire about your grandfather's health."

Behind him, the blue roan nudged his hand and he affectionately curled his arm around the horse's nose and tucked it against his side.

"So how is Gramps doing?"

"I'm proud of him. He's trying very hard."

"Gramps never was a quitter. Has he been giving you a hard time?"

The way he asked the question made it sound as though he'd be glad to intervene on her behalf. Like a gallant knight ready to defend her. The notion touched her and she couldn't stop a small smile from curling her lips.

"Contrary to what you or others might think, your grandfather has been very sweet to me. Even when I'm ordering him to do more."

Disbelief appeared in his eyes. "Dad implied you were a miracle worker. He must be right."

She shouldn't let his casual compliment affect her, but it did. Her job was her life. To be praised for her effort, even by Rafe Calhoun, felt good.

He and Roscoe drew closer and suddenly Lilly couldn't keep her eyes off him. There was something so vibrant and male about his rugged features that she forgot to breathe and very nearly forgot to think.

"Thanks, but I'm just doing my job," she told him. "And your grandfather and I just happened to hit it off."

Leaning his head through the open window, he said, "Well, actually, I had another motive for stopping you."

For some ridiculous reason her gaze settled on his lips and immediately the image of kissing him danced into her thoughts. Would he taste as rough and tough and male as he looked? she wondered. Oh, Lord, she had to quit looking. Had to quit fantasizing.

"And what was that?" she asked.

He grinned and Lilly decided the slightly crooked line of his teeth matched the rest of him. Raw, natural and untamed.

"I wanted to let you know that I took your advice and had a talk with the man in the mirror. But he didn't know a Romeo."

"You're incorrigible!"

He chuckled. "I can dance, too. Why don't we go out this evening and I'll show you?"

Inwardly groaning, she asked herself how she'd managed to get herself into this predicament. Instead of stopping on the road, she should've floored the gas pedal and left the man and his horse in the dust.

"Sorry, but I have to work tonight."

"Okay, then tomorrow night," he persisted.

"I have to work then, too."

He rolled his eyes. "Is there a night you don't have to work?"

If she lied about her work schedule, she might stand a chance of getting rid of this man's attentions once and for all. But lying to Rafe didn't appeal to her and if she was being totally honest with herself, she didn't want to get rid of him. For the first time in years, he was making her feel excited. Making her remember that she was more than a nurse; she was a woman.

Her heart suddenly jumped into a fast, reckless rhythm. "Monday is my night off."

"Great! I'll pick you up at seven."

She gave him her address, then seeing he had no way to write it down, she asked, "Will you remember that?"

"Don't worry. I'll find you."

Lifting a hand in farewell, he moved away from the car and swung himself into the saddle and all Lilly could do was watch him gallop away. What was she getting herself into? she wondered.

And why couldn't she resist finding out…?

## Chapter Two

For the next three days, Lilly vacillated between wanting to kick herself or pat herself on the back for being brave enough to accept a date with Rafe Calhoun.

Since the morning he'd run her down on the road, like some scene out of a Western movie, she'd fought against the urge to ask around about the man. Most people in her circle of friends and coworkers didn't rub elbows with the rich Calhoun family, so whatever they told her about Rafe would be little more than hearsay.

Ironically, she was the only one who'd had any actual association to the family. Seven years ago, Rafe's mother, Claudia, had befriended her when she'd desperately needed someone to lean on. Lilly had never told anyone about the chance meeting between her and the matriarch of the Silver Horn ranch, or the friendship that had resulted from it. That time in her life was too painful to share with anyone. And Claudia had since died.

But Lilly's friendship with the woman still lived in her heart and that had been the main reason she'd agreed to take on the job of Bart Calhoun's therapy.

Normally, the hands of the clock spun too quickly for Lilly. Work kept her rushing to find enough time in the day to get necessary chores around the house done and errands about town completed. But as Monday evening arrived, it felt to Lilly as though time began to crawl.

By the time Rafe finally arrived a few minutes before seven, she'd worked herself up into a nervous frenzy. But in spite of her nerves, she did her best to appear cool and collected when she answered the door.

"Good evening, Lilly."

"Hello, Rafe. Would you like to come in?"

"I'd love to."

She opened the door wider and as he stepped over the threshold Lilly was a bit overwhelmed by the change in his appearance. Instead of worn chaps and a battered hat, he was dressed in dark, Western-cut slacks. A crisp white shirt was buttoned at his throat and topped with a bolo tie fashioned from a turquoise rock, while a black felt hat dangled from his hand. If James Bond were a cowboy, he'd have to look like Rafe, Lilly decided.

He handed her a long, slim box full of expensive chocolates. "I hope you like sweets."

"Unfortunately, I love them. Thank you." She put the box down on a nearby coffee table then gestured for him to take a seat. "Do we have time for a drink? I have tea or coffee. But nothing to make a cocktail."

"If I'd known you were going to be this hospitable I would have made a point of coming earlier," he joked, then pushed back the cuff of his shirt to peer at a gold watch on his wrist. "But I don't want us to lose our reservations. I'll take a rain check on the drink, if you don't mind."

"Surely. Just let me get my bag and wrap."

She left for the bedroom and when she returned with her things, Rafe was standing in front of a wall table where several photos of family and friends were arranged on a white lace doily.

"Is this your parents?" he asked, pointing to one particular photo.

"Yes. About twenty years ago."

"And that's you in the middle?"

A wan smile touched her lips. "That's me. I was eight years old there—a chubby little tomboy. Back then I had the burning desire to be the first girl to play major league baseball."

Instead of raising a chuckle out of him, he turned a curious look on her. "You've surprised me. I would've never figured you for a rough-and-tumble girl like that."

She shrugged. "Well, I grew up and decided to aim for less lofty goals. I still love baseball, though. Do you like sports?"

"Never have time for them," he admitted. "But Sassy, my younger half sister, has talked about playing in a softball league back when she lived in New Mexico. I need to introduce you to her. You two might have a lot in common."

Surprised, she said, "I wasn't aware that you had a sister."

A faint smile touched his lips. "It's a long story. I'll tell you all about it some time. Right now we'd better be going."

He made it sound as though they'd be spending more time together in the future and though the idea was tantalizing, Lilly wasn't sure she could allow that to happen. One night with this man was going to be hard enough to get through and still keep her resistance intact.

Outside, the evening air had already begun to cool and before they stepped off the small porch, Lilly took a moment to wrap a white shawl around her bare shoulders.

"Have you lived here long?" Rafe asked as he took her by the elbow and started to his waiting truck.

"Yes. I bought the place a few years ago. It's nothing fancy, but it's not far from work and my neighbors are very nice." The modest, two-bedroom house sat on two lots surrounded by chain-link fence. Except for a large cottonwood and a tall patch of prickly pear near the porch, the yard was mostly bare of landscape. "I've been planning to do more with the yard, but being a nurse always seems to get in the way of planting shrubs and flowers."

"I like it this way," he said. "Nice and neat."

Compared to the Silver Horn ranch house, this place must look like a miniature dollhouse to him, but then compared to his home, most every house in Carson City was lacking.

His vehicle, a sleek, black, four-door pickup truck was parked along the street and as he helped her into the passenger seat, he said, "I hope you don't mind riding in a truck. We've not had a car on the ranch since—not in a long time."

Lilly wondered if he was going to say since his mother had passed away. But she wasn't going to ask. Not when he'd clearly skirted the issue.

"I don't mind," she assured him.

And why would she? The interior of Rafe's truck was far more luxurious than her little economy car or, for that matter, anything she'd ever ridden in. The seats were buttery-soft leather and the dashboard was equipped with all sorts of gadgets that she would need a manual to operate.

Rafe and his four brothers had been born into wealth and she wondered if he took all the luxury for granted, or if that aspect of his life was even important to him.

The questions made her realize how very little she knew about this man. But then she didn't want to get to know him that well. She wanted to keep this evening light and simple. And once it was over she could put it and him behind her.

"So how was your day?" he asked as they traveled down a residential street that would connect them to a main thoroughfare.

"Restful. After working eighty hours this past week in E.R. a day off is special. The only nursing I did today was with your grandfather."

"You drove out to the Horn on your day off just to give Gramps his therapy? You must be damned dedicated."

"Bart is making such good progress that I don't want to miss a day. At least, not until he reaches another level."

"He showed me how he can work his fingers now. I was impressed. You've only been treating him for a week."

"Two weeks," she corrected. "I had already been working with Bart a week before that day you and I met on the stairs."

With a rueful shake of his head, he said, "What a shame. All that wasted time that we could have had together."

Ignoring his outrageous comment, she said, "Apparently, you don't spend much time around the house."

"I sleep and eat there, but not much more. I have too many responsibilities outside," he explained. "There's always something to be done on the range—with the cattle and horses."

She glanced over at him and was instantly struck by his long, lean body and the dark, proud profile of his face. The only cowboys she'd ever been around were the ones who passed through the E.R. and the common denominator she'd noticed in them was their gritty toughness. She expected Rafe Calhoun was the epitome of that.

"And what exactly are your responsibilities on the ranch?"

"I'm the foreman over the cow/calf operation. I oversee the health and nutrition of all the cattle and that includes every aspect of their feeding routine, conditions of the grazing land, calving operations, breeding, identification and vaccination. There's more, but I don't want to bore you."

"It doesn't bore me at all. Since I know very little about ranching, it's all fascinating to me."

He slanted her a wry look. "It's hard to imagine that you aren't familiar with ranching. You live in the West, my dear. Where do you hang out?"

"There are several hospitals in Carson City. Are you familiar with nursing and medical treatment?" she tossed back at him.

He chuckled. "You are good, Lilly. Real good. I have the feeling you're going to keep me on my toes tonight."

And she had a feeling she was already in trouble, Lilly decided. Not only was the man a delight to her eyes, he made her want to smile. Something that Lilly had almost forgotten how to do.

"I'll try not to be a dull girl," she promised, then

glanced around as she noticed the bulk of the city slipping behind them. "I thought we were going to eat. What do you have planned? Parking out on the desert and eating off the tailgate?"

He snapped his fingers. "Say, that's a nice idea. Especially with the moon almost being full. But unfortunately, I didn't think of it before I made reservations at a place over on the north rim of the lake."

She'd not expected him to drive all the way to Lake Tahoe just for dinner. But she supposed it didn't really matter. Whether they were in a fast-food joint or a cozy café, she was going to be in his close company and she could already feel that each moment she spent with this man was going to take a heavy toll on her common sense.

A half hour later, when he pulled the truck to a stop in front of the Sierra Chateau and handed the keys to a waiting valet, Lilly was beginning to understand just what it meant to be a Calhoun. The closest that she, or any of her friends, had gotten to this place was only in their imagination.

The three-story rock structure resembled a small castle nestled within giant pines and pungent spruce trees. A rock bridge formed a walkway over a rushing stream while every space of lawn was filled with blooming shrubs and flowers. It was truly a fairy-tale scene.

"Rafe, I'm very angry with you," she said as he tucked her hand into the curve of his arm.

He escorted her over the bridge toward a canopied entrance where a doorman waited to open a pair of opulent glass doors. "Why? I haven't done anything—yet."

"I am not dressed for anything like this! And I don't

think I'll be comfortable. Why couldn't we have gone out for burgers and fries?"

He thumped the heel of his palm against his forehead in a clueless gesture. "Why in heck didn't you tell me beforehand?"

"Because you didn't give me a chance to tell you anything. You simply took the bull by the horns."

His eyes sparkling, he grinned down at her. "I am a cowboy," he reminded her. "I'm an expert at taking the bull by the horns."

Lilly figured he was an expert at taking, all right. Anything he happened to want. The trick was to make darn sure that what he wanted wasn't her.

"Quit worrying, Lilly. You look gorgeous. And I brought you here to enjoy the evening. We'll do burgers next time."

She wasn't going to think about a next time. It was going to be hard enough just to survive the night.

Inside the lavish restaurant, a hostess quickly ushered them to a beautiful little table with a view of the lake. As they waited for their meal, Lilly sipped on ginger ale while Rafe enjoyed a locally brewed lager. Nearby, several couples were quietly dining and Lilly tried not to notice how all the women were impeccably dressed.

Even though her white silk top and black pencil skirt were acceptable, she felt completely underdressed. Yet from the appreciative way Rafe's gaze kept sliding over her, he seemed to think she looked perfect. The notion made her want to squirm upon the wide, padded chair. Sure, she liked for men to think she was attractive, but Rafe was eyeing her as though he wanted to have her for dinner, rather than the prime rib he'd ordered.

"Tell me, Lilly, have you always lived in Carson City?"

"No. Up until I was three years old, we lived in St. George, Utah, but then my father's job was transferred to Nevada. He's a welder for the Virginia-Truckee railroad. My parents live just outside of Virginia City."

"So your parents are still together? Nowadays that's quite a feat."

It was definitely a feat for Faye and Ron, she thought dourly. But she wasn't about to delve into the problems her parents had endured in their marriage. She hated to even think of their battles, much less share them with someone like Rafe. His mother had been full of compassion and quiet, gentle grace whereas Faye was impatient, loud and critical. He wouldn't understand a woman like Lilly's mother. There were times that Lilly didn't understand her, either, but in spite of Faye's shortcomings, she loved her.

She grimaced. "It's pretty miraculous, all right."

He lifted the glass of beer to his lips and after a long drink, he said, "I understand you've met my dad, Orin. Has anyone told you that my mother died a few years ago?"

"No one had to tell me," she informed him. "I was actually acquainted with Claudia. In fact, I attended her funeral services."

For the first time since she'd met him, she saw a look of real surprise cross his face, which was immediately followed by a dark, almost brooding shadow.

"You knew my mother? I never expected that."

She nodded while her gaze followed the movement of his hands as he placed the glass down on the tabletop. All night long, her eyes had kept returning to his long, tanned fingers with their short, clipped nails. He had strong hands with rough palms that caused a buzz of excitement each time they touched her skin. The thought of them moving over her with passion also had her wondering just how many women had experienced the touch of those hands and how many more he'd lured into his bed.

"Claudia used to volunteer at Tahoe General. We—uh—would bump into each other from time to time. She was a lovely woman inside and out. I was so shocked when she took that fall in her home. But all the staff at the hospital expected her to fully recover."

His gaze dropped to the tabletop. "It was all so senseless, Lilly. She was carrying a basket of laundry down the stairs and took a bad step. We've always had maids for that sort of thing. There wasn't any need for her to be doing it—but that's the way she was—always busy and working." He shook his head as though the whole incident was still hard for him to believe or accept. "The fall gave her a concussion, but she appeared to get over it quickly. She'd been discharged from the hospital and was back to her normal routine when she just collapsed and we couldn't revive her. A blood clot had developed in her brain."

"I can't imagine how much that must have hurt you and your whole family," she said. "The only family members I've lost were my elderly grandfathers and they'd both been ill for a long time. So their passing was expected."

Rafe looked up and she could see how just talking about his mother had drained the sparkle from his gray eyes. His reaction made her wonder if he'd had an extra-close relationship with her.

"Once she was gone, nothing was ever the same." He looked off, his expression pensive. "I don't normally talk about when Mom died. Not to anyone. But you're a nurse. You understand. And I like you, Lilly."

As he spoke the last words, his gaze returned to hers, and Lilly felt her heart wince with a mixture of emotions. She'd not expected anything so serious to come out of Rafe's mouth. He was a flirt and playboy. He was all about having fun. It was jarring to learn that he could hurt and feel as deeply as any poor, old Joe.

"I'm not sure I understand any better than you why good people get injured or ill. Sometimes I go home from a long night of work and wonder what I'm doing. Sometimes I even tell myself I'm going to walk away from nursing and do something that won't tear my heart apart." Sighing, she reached for her glass. "But in the end I can't. I want to help people."

A waitress arrived with their salads and they readied themselves to eat before Rafe picked up the conversation again.

"I'm curious as to what made you want to be a nurse. It's an admirable profession, but the workload and the stress would be hard for most people to handle."

"My grandmother, my father's mom, has been a nurse for close to forty years. She's sixty-seven now and still working at a hospital in Henderson."

"Wow. That's dedication. Is she married?"

Lilly nodded. "Why? Are you looking for an older woman for yourself? One that could nurse you back to health if need be?" she teased. "From my experience in E.R. you cowboys are always suffering cuts, broken bones and torn ligaments."

He grinned. "We do take some spills. But your grandmother sounds like the perfect wife for Dad. Not that he's looking. But a couple of my brothers are looking for him."

Lilly seriously doubted that Rafe was looking for a wife, either. But that hardly mattered to her. This was just an evening out. Nothing more. Nothing less.

"Grandma is special. From the time I was a little girl she was my heroine and still is. She's steady as a rock, compassionate, yet firm when she has to be. One day I hope to be as good a nurse as she is."

"Dad told me that you don't work in therapy anymore—you work in the E.R. That's quite a switch, isn't it?"

She forked a piece of romaine lettuce. "I like the unexpected. And in the E.R. you never know what's going to show up."

His gaze slipped over her face. "So you're a girl who likes excitement."

She'd never thought of herself in those terms, but he must be right, otherwise she would've never agreed to this date.

"I'd rather think I'm a girl who likes a challenge," she said wryly.

He chuckled. "Then you ought to like me, Lilly. A whole lot."

More than an hour later, after coffee and a rich, decadent dessert, Rafe ushered Lilly into the club side of the restaurant where a long bar and several small tables gave way to a spacious dance floor.

To one side of the dance area, an elevated platform in the shape of a half circle held a six-piece band. At the microphone, a woman with long black hair and a clingy red evening gown was belting out a torchy standard from the 1950s.

Not bothering with a table, Rafe led her straight to the dance floor and pulled her into his arms. At first, she kept a rigid distance away from him, but after he applied a gentle pressure against her back, she finally surrendered. And as her curves melted against him, he decided there was something very unique about Lilly Lockett. She was making him think about her instead of himself and all that needed to be done on the ranch in the coming days.

"Now that is my kind of music," he said as he nuzzled his cheek against the side of her blond hair. "Bluesy and soulful."

"I thought you cowboys were all guitars and twang."

"Hmm. We're not cookie cutter, Lilly. I have three or four wranglers who love rock music. They turn the radio up so loud in the work trucks it blasts my eardrums. A few more like standards and one even goes for classical stuff. But there are country and western fans among the bunch, too. We're an eclectic group."

"There goes my vision of you sitting around the campfire singing trail songs."

He chuckled and then went quiet as the sheer pleasure of having her in his arms took over his senses. She smelled like some sort of flower. A gardenia, he guessed, or maybe it was a rose. The only thing he knew about flowers was that a bunch of them could usually smooth an angry woman. And he'd dealt with plenty of those in his lifetime. Especially when he grew tired of one and didn't take pains to give her a gentle send-off. Funny, but he couldn't imagine himself getting tired of this one. She was beautiful and quick and something about her made him feel so damned protective. And that wasn't like him. Not like him, at all.

"Do you come here often?"

Her question broke into his thoughts and he peered

down at the shiny crown of her head. Her hair was like spun sunlight, all soft and golden. The morning he'd first spotted her on the stairs it had been confined in a bun at the back of her head. But tonight it was loose and curled ever so slightly against her shoulders, while a jagged fringe brushed her eyebrows. All evening he'd been itching to get his fingers into it and now that he had her close, he dared to roll a strand between his thumb and forefinger.

"I rarely come here," he answered.

Her head tilted back in order to study his face. "Then why did you bring me?"

"I wanted to do something nice for you," he admitted.

She reasoned, "You hardly know me."

"I'm learning more by the minute," he told her. "For one thing, your hair doesn't feel a bit like Roscoe's mane."

"Mine's coarser, I'm sure."

He chuckled. "Since you're a nurse, you might be interested to know that Roscoe's tail hair makes great sutures."

She frowned with disbelief. "You're kidding now."

He held up a hand. "Scout's honor. If I'm lying, I'm dying. I can't count the times I've used it to sew up a cow or calf out on the range."

"I would've guessed that the Silver Horn had a resident vet to do those sorts of things."

"The Horn does have a resident vet, but he can't be over thousands of acres at once. You find a hurt animal five, ten miles away from the ranch yard, you do your best to take care of it yourself. Of course, if the injury is really serious, the animal has to be transported back to the barns."

She smiled up at him and Rafe felt his heart give a

ridiculous little jerk. What the hell was the matter with him? he wondered. Women smiled at him all the time and he enjoyed the attention. But his heart sure didn't go pitter-patter. At least, it hadn't until this very minute.

She said, "Looks like I'm learning things tonight, too."

The song suddenly came to an end and rather than wait for the music to begin again, Rafe said, "Let's go out on the balcony and look at the lake."

"All right," she agreed. "But I should warn you that I'll need to be heading home soon. I have to be up early in the morning."

"I'd like to argue with you about that. But for once, I'll be a nice guy. We'll stay for only a few more minutes. I don't want to make you tired and grumpy in the morning."

With his hand clamped around hers, he led her through the dancers and out onto the wide balcony that was an extension of the dance floor. As they leaned against the tall railing, the cool night air prompted Rafe to pull her shawl up on her shoulders, but it was the warmth of her skin seeping through the thin fabric that made his hands linger there.

"Oh, the moon looks so gorgeous hanging over the water." She let out an appreciative sigh. "It makes it look like liquid silver."

"I'm glad you're enjoying the view."

"It's a far cry from the emergency room," she admitted.

"And you're a far cry from the branding lot."

That brought her head around to his and Rafe's gaze barely had time to connect with hers before it fell to her parted lips. The pink, moist curves sent a shaft of longing right through him.

"Now I suppose you're going to say that I look so beautiful in the moonlight that you just have to kiss me."

Her jaded tone told him that she'd been disappointed by one or more men in her life. It also told him that she wasn't a naive girl that he could easily wrap around his finger. But then, Rafe wasn't sure he'd want to do that, even if he could. He was smart enough to know that Lilly wasn't the type of woman a man could make love to then simply walk away. And he was the walk-away type. He didn't want the fuss or complication of having one special woman in his life. Besides, he was already married to the ranch. He didn't have room in his heart for a woman.

"Actually, I was going to say the moonlight makes your hair look like silver, too." He thrust his fingers into the soft, blond waves and dipped his face close to hers. But your idea is better. Much better."

"It wasn't an idea—it was—"

Her words stopped as his lips hovered over hers.

"Was what?" he prompted.

She turned her face away from his and stared out at the lake.

"Men like you have all the cheesy lines—all the slick moves," she said flatly. "It doesn't impress me. It bores me."

"Then maybe this won't."

Without giving her time to guess his intentions, he tugged her face around to his. Surprise flashed in her eyes, but it didn't stop Rafe from lowering his mouth to hers. He had to kiss her. Had to show her exactly the sort of man she was dealing with. A man who would never be her pushover.

## Chapter Three

Somewhere in the middle of the kiss or after it had ended, Rafe wasn't sure which, the realization that he was in trouble struck him hard. This wasn't the way any of it was supposed to go, he thought.

He was supposed to be feeling triumphant and smug and she was supposed to be swooning in his arms. Instead, she was staring at him as though she couldn't decide whether she wanted to slap him or run a dagger through him.

"If that was a sample of your charms, then I'd advise you to save them for some unsuspecting woman. And that isn't me."

She stepped around him and Rafe had little choice but to follow her. Once they were inside, he quickly settled the bill and in a matter of a few short minutes the two of them were in his truck, traveling back to Carson City.

During the whole process, Lilly said very little and

for once, Rafe couldn't come up with anything useful to say. How could he? He'd never dated a woman like Lilly. His usual glibness wouldn't have the same effect on her.

*Maybe you should try open honesty, Rafe. That would be a refreshing change.*

The voice in his head had him scowling as he stared at the dark highway in front of him. Being honest with a woman would get him into far more trouble than an unwanted kiss.

"I don't know why you're frowning, Rafe. Up until that kiss, I had a lovely evening."

That jerked his head around and for a split second, he forgot about keeping his eyes on the highway. "Just exactly what was wrong with that kiss?"

"As far as kisses go, it was very pleasant. But I didn't ask for it. That's what was wrong."

Rafe wasn't accustomed to asking for anything. Whatever he wanted, he took. Clearly, that wasn't going to work with Lilly.

"I'm sorry," he said in a mollified tone. "Can you forgive me?"

"Of course I can. I already have."

It was downright silly at how much her words perked his spirits.

"You can—you have?"

"Why wouldn't I? I don't hold grudges. Besides, since I have no intention of kissing you again, none of this really matters. So I apologize for getting a little testy with you."

"Oh, Lilly, that's—" Totally confused by her attitude, he glanced over to see she was staring out the passenger window instead of at him. That wasn't a good sign. "Why aren't you going to kiss me again?"

She sighed. "Look, Rafe, I agreed to this date because I knew you wouldn't give up on a challenge. I figured once we'd gone out you'd see we wouldn't suit and you'd be on to the next girl. I thought that would make everything easier, because you're just not my kind of guy."

He couldn't remember any woman ever telling him that. But instead of making him feel angry or humiliated, he was more perplexed than anything.

"What is your kind of guy, Lilly? One who spends his evenings at home quietly reading the newspaper and saying yes, dear or no, dear?"

Long moments passed before she finally answered, "Could be that's exactly what I'm looking for."

He muttered a curse under his breath. "Sure. This from a woman who chose to give up therapy to work in the E.R. Yeah, you want a dull man, all right."

"Don't try to figure out what I want, Rafe. You might hurt yourself."

She was right about that. He needed to give her a quick goodbye and never even glance in the rearview mirror. She was the kind of woman who could cause a man a deep-down hurt and he hardly needed more pain in his life.

Rafe was still telling himself that when ten minutes later, he parked the truck in front of Lilly's house and helped her to the ground. But the touch of her hand upon his arm as he walked her to the door made it very difficult to concentrate on the mental warning.

When they reached the porch, she said, "I did offer you a drink before we left this evening. The offer still holds if you'd like a coffee. Just as a thank-you for the nice meal. Nothing else."

Normally, he would have jumped at the chance to

spend more time with this woman. Especially since she was being nice enough to invite him into her home. But to be honest with himself, he was feeling a little more than rattled. Some of the things she'd said had left him bruised and raw.

"Thanks, but I'll take a rain check. You have to be up early and I've got a long day ahead of me tomorrow."

She smiled at him and for one split second, Rafe wondered if he'd lost his mind.

She raised up on tiptoes and placed a kiss against his cheek. "Thank you for the dinner and the dancing. It was very nice."

"My pleasure, Lilly." He pressed her hand between his. "Good night."

"Good night, Rafe."

He turned and quickly walked to his truck, but as he drove away he couldn't stop himself from looking back. And as he watched her step into the house and close the door behind her, he felt an inexplicable loss. One that he'd never expected to be feeling after a date with a beautiful woman.

The next morning when Lilly arrived at the Silver Horn to treat Bart, she didn't see Rafe anywhere around the ranch yard. And more than an hour later, when she drove away, there was no Wild West show of him and Roscoe running her down and stopping her on the road.

She told herself she was glad that she'd not had to encounter the man, especially after that kiss last night. But if she was being honest with herself, she felt a little deflated that, at the very least, he'd not been around to say hello.

*And why should he want to waste his time just to say*

*hello to you, Lilly? You were rough on him last night. Unreasonably so. The man isn't Grant Winters. You shouldn't be treating him like the man who broke your heart.*

The voice in her head haunted her all the way back to Carson City and by the time she'd put in four hours of work in the emergency room she was still thinking about Rafe and the night before.

When things finally slowed enough for her to take her first break, she went to the snack room and pulled out her cell phone. She didn't have Rafe's personal number, but she had Bart's. The elder Calhoun would no doubt pass his grandson's number on to her. Even though Rafe had irked her with his trite advances, she should've reacted with more ladylike, respectable manners.

Bart answered after the second ring and after she quickly identified herself, he said, "Lilly, you don't have to check up on me. I'm exercising my hand right this minute."

"I'm not checking up, Bart. I trust you completely. I'm calling to ask a favor. Could you possibly give me Rafe's cell-phone number?"

Even though the man couldn't see her, she could feel a blush wash over her face. *Silly, silly Lilly,* she scolded herself.

"Sure can. Just give me a minute to find the little book where I keep all my names and numbers."

Several moments passed while she could hear papers being shuffled and a drawer being opened and closed. Finally, he came back to the phone. "Here it is, Lilly. But before I give it to you, can I ask why you want my grandson's number? You're not planning to discuss me behind my back, are you?"

Lilly laughed at that idea. "No, Bart. I promise that whatever I need to say to you, I'll say it right to your face."

"Oh. Well, I wasn't aware that you were acquainted with Rafe."

"We've—uh—spent a little time together."

He grunted with disapproval. "Aw, Lilly. That boy isn't for you. He's naughty. He's got too much of me in him. Understand?"

The fact that Bart cared enough about her to give her the simple warning was enough to make her smile. "Don't worry. It's nothing serious. I just need to give him a message, that's all."

"Okay. I won't preach at you anymore."

He gave her the number and after scratching it down on a small square of paper, Lilly thanked him, then quickly ended the call.

"Hey, got anything in here to eat?"

Lilly stuffed the piece of paper with the number into the pocket on her white uniform just as Marcella, a fellow E.R. nurse, walked into the small snack room.

"I've not even had time to get coffee, much less something to eat," Lilly told her. "I put a sandwich in the fridge if you want half of it."

The tall, auburn-haired woman shook her head as she walked over to the coffee machine and filled a foam cup. "I was just kidding. I splurged this morning and stopped at the bakery. I'll have to starve myself for the rest of the day just to make up for the apple fritter I devoured."

Marcella was in her early thirties, divorced and the mother of a five-year-old son. She was an excellent nurse and one of the few good friends that Lilly could always count on.

"Don't be starving yourself," Lilly scolded her. "There's enough sick people around here without us having to scrape you off the floor. Besides, you always look great."

"Yeah. Yeah," Marcella teased. "You must want me to work a shift for you."

"No. Just being honest." She rose from the table to pour herself a cup of coffee. "But it would be nice to have a whole week off. I can't remember the last time I got six hours of sleep."

Frowning thoughtfully, Marcella said, "I thought you were off last night."

Lilly stared into her coffee cup. "I was. But I went on a date."

Marcella gasped. "A date! My Lord, knock a board off the house!"

Blowing out an exasperated breath, Lilly looked up to see Marcella's mouth gaping open. "Just hush. You're making me sound like a freak or something."

Marcella jerked one of the metal chairs from beneath the table and sank onto the edge. "Tell me. Who? Why? Where?"

Lilly sipped her coffee more as a stalling tactic than a desire for more of the half-burned brew. "Rafe Calhoun took me to the Sierra Chateau for dinner. That's all."

If Marcella had looked surprised a moment ago, she looked completely stunned now. "That's all! How did this happen?"

With a negligible shrug, Lilly said, "We met on the ranch while I was there for Bart's therapy session. He asked me for a date and I accepted. It was a spur-of-the-moment sort of thing. Nothing is going to come of it. I can assure you of that."

"Really? What makes you so certain nothing will come of it?"

Grimacing, she tossed the remainder of her coffee in a trash bin. "Because I've already made it clear to him that one date was all I would agree to. Anyway, he's not into serious, Marcella. Besides, he's a Calhoun. Even if he was looking for a wife, he wouldn't search among simple, hardworking women like me."

"Hmm. Well, from what I've heard, he's the playboy of the Calhoun boys. I saw him here at the hospital the night they brought the old man in with a stroke. He's a long, lean hunk of man. So are his brothers."

A sigh unwittingly escaped Lilly. She had to agree that Rafe was one attractive, sexy male. But there was much more to him than his looks and his wealth. Last night she was just beginning to see a different side of him and then he'd had to go and ruin it all with that kiss.

*And just why had that kiss ruined it, Lilly? Because you enjoyed it? Because for the first time in years you felt something flicker inside you and you were terrified?*

"I honestly don't know anything about those rumors concerning Rafe and women," Lilly said. "But after spending an evening with him I have a feeling most of the rumors are probably true. And you know how I feel about guys like that."

Marcella shot her a tired look. "You mean guys like Grant, don't you?"

Pushing away from the cabinet she'd been leaning against, Lilly said, "I don't want to discuss that bastard now or ever."

Shaking her head, Marcella said, "Okay. But don't punish the rest of the male population because of one rat-fink doctor. Rafe Calhoun might be the perfect man for you—if you'd give him a chance."

Lilly's short laugh was caustic. "Sure. About like you and I are going to spend the next two hours sitting around twiddling our thumbs. It ain't gonna happen."

She'd hardly gotten the words out of her mouth when the intercom over their heads sounded off, ending the women's short break.

"All nurses in examining room two. All nurses needed in emergency room two."

Exchanging pointed glances, the two women hurried away to answer the call.

Two days later, just before dark, Rafe had showered and changed into clean clothes, when he checked the cell phone he'd left charging on the dresser top.

After spending the past couple of days working out on the range, the phone's battery had died a quick death and without electricity or even a truck to charge it, he'd been out of touch with civilization. Which was okay with him. Three-fourths of the calls he received were trivial, or from someone he didn't want to speak to in the first place.

As he scrolled through the call log, he expected to find mostly garbage, so it was a complete shock to see Lilly's name by one of the numbers. She'd only given him the cell number in case he needed to call and postpone or cancel their date. And he didn't have a clue as to how she'd gotten his number.

Lilly? He hurriedly scanned the call for a date. She'd called him two evenings ago! And he'd not even known it!

Crossing over to the bed, he sank onto the edge of the mattress and stared thoughtfully at the phone. His first instinct was to call her number now, this very instant. But did he really want to do that?

Ever since he'd driven away from her house a few nights ago, he'd been trying to convince himself that she wasn't the type of woman he needed to go after. If she cooked breakfast for a man, she'd want to be wearing a wedding band while she flipped his pancakes. And he didn't want a wife. A wife would bind him in ties that would choke him. A wife meant loving and protecting. And all the while worrying that he might lose her in some awful, unpredictable way.

Rafe had only been five years old when his little sister Darci died from an untreatable heart disease. Born three years after him, she'd been a fragile little thing with a mop of russet-colored curls and big green eyes. Even to this day, Rafe could remember her giggles and how she would hold tightly on to his hand, and cry if she didn't get chocolate milk for breakfast.

He'd adored Darci and losing her had both confused and scared him. For months after her death, Rafe had been terrified that his brothers might leave him in the same way and he'd wanted to cling to his mother for a sense of security. He'd been too young to understand that she'd also been dealing with her own sorrow.

Thankfully, the passing years had dimmed his grief and as he'd grown into a man, he'd lost the incessant fear of losing another family member. Tragedy had struck the Calhoun family once; he couldn't imagine it striking a second time. Then an accident had taken his mother and suddenly the direction of everything he'd ever wanted in life took a drastic change.

Rafe had watched the light of happiness disappear from his father's eyes and the only home Rafe had ever known had taken on a chill that, to this day, was still present.

From that point on, Rafe had decided he'd never have a family of his own and that decision hadn't changed. No. Rafe didn't want that for himself. There were plenty of men out there who'd make a fine husband for Lilly, who'd be willing to take on the risks and responsibilities of having a family. But damn it, the thought of her with another man made make him sick.

Shutting his mind from those thoughts, Rafe took a closer glance at the phone and spotted a voice mail notification. Could it be from Lilly? He punched the symbol, then lifted the phone to his ear.

*"Hi, Rafe. It's Lilly. I hope you don't mind that I got your number from Bart. I was just calling to say—well, I want to apologize for my behavior the other night. That wasn't really me. And I was rough on you for all the wrong reasons. I did have a nice time. And the kiss was—nice, too."*

The message ended without a "goodbye" or "call me," but it was enough to make Rafe jump straight to his feet and start jamming the tails of his shirt into his jeans.

Cold one minute and hot the next. Rafe didn't know which one was the real Lilly Lockett. But he was damned sure going to find out.

Shortly after eight o'clock that night, Lilly and Marcella ended their shift and were leaving the building together. On the way to the parking lot, Marcella was still voicing her concerns over a small boy they had treated for an asthma attack.

"Lilly, I'm telling you I think social services needs to visit that boy's home. Something just doesn't feel right about the whole situation. He looks half-starved. And this is the second time he's been treated in the past two weeks. I don't think his parents are even bothering to feed him, much less see that he takes his medication."

"Someone bothered enough to bring him to the hospital," Lilly pointed out.

"A grandfather—I think. And he looked too feeble to care for himself. I'm surprised he managed to drive the child here to emergency. Oh, God, Lilly, he's my Harry's age. And I just want to take him in my arms and carry him home with me."

Lilly patted her friend's shoulder. "Marcella, don't worry. We'll go to Doctor Malloy and explain our fears about the child to him. He'll contact the right people."

Her friend nodded somberly. "You're right. If we don't go through the proper channels, getting the boy some real help might backfire. I'm going home and try not to think about it tonight."

Lilly gave her a weary smile. "Good. Give Harry a kiss and be thankful you have him."

"I will. Good night," Marcella told her, then broke away to go to her car that was parked at the other end of the parking area.

After waving her friend off, Lilly fished the car keys from the tote bag she was carrying and pushed the button to unlock the doors. She was about to climb beneath the steering wheel when a male voice sounded directly behind her, causing her to jump with fright.

With a hand clutched to her chest, she whirled around to see Rafe standing a few steps away. He was dressed all in denim and a black hat shaded his face from what little light there was from the streetlamps, but she could see enough of his features to tell there was a faint grin on his face.

"Rafe! What are you doing here?"

He moved closer. "Waiting on you to get off work. I asked at the nurses' desk to speak with you, but a nurse there told me you were busy changing shifts and that you'd be out shortly."

She let out a long, pent-up breath. "I—well, you certainly surprised me. Is anything wrong with Bart? He seemed fine this morning."

Shaking his head, he took another step toward her. "Gramps is fine. I just found your voice mail earlier this evening. My men and I have been working out on the far west range for the past two days. My phone lost its charge."

"Oh. I had decided you didn't want to talk to me."

He continued to study her closely. "The other night before I left your house, you implied that I was wasting my time with you. Am I?"

Reaching up, she pulled a pin from her coiled hair and shook it free. "I honestly don't know, Rafe. The other night—I was—well, I rarely date. You see, I made a mistake in trusting a man once and since then I'm afraid I see most of you as predators. That's wrong of me, I know. But I can't get past it."

He was close enough now for her to see his features soften and a look of understanding flicker in his eyes.

"Lilly."

As he spoke her name his hands reached out to cradle her face, and his touch was like a ray of sunlight bathing every cell in her body with delicious heat.

"I'm not going to pretend that I'm the perfect guy for you. Or that I'm even a good guy. I only know that when

I'm with you everything feels different. I feel different. Something about being with you brings out the better side of me. I don't want that to end, Lilly."

The quiver she felt rushing through her body had nothing to do with being exhausted and everything to do with this man that was touching her as tenderly as a drop of dew on a rose petal.

"These past few days I've been trying not to think about you, Rafe. But to be honest, I've missed you."

He didn't make any sort of reply. Instead, he threaded his fingers into her hair, then bent his head toward hers. The second his lips angled over hers, the cautious side of her was screaming for her to step back and run from this man. But the lonely yearning inside her was much stronger and before she knew it, she was slipping her arms around his waist and opening her mouth to his eager kiss.

After that, she was totally and completely lost. His sensual scent swirled through her head and mingled with the taste of his mouth. Against her back, she could feel his hands drawing her closer and closer. Sweet, hot desire burst inside her and the onslaught had her desperately clutching his arms for support.

The kiss went on and on and probably would have continued if it hadn't been for the sound of approaching voices. When their mouths finally tore apart, Lilly quickly stepped back to put a respectable distance between them. As she sucked long breaths of air into her starved lungs, she realized her lips were burning and so was the rest of her body.

Taking her by the hand, Rafe said in a low, husky voice, "Let's go somewhere for coffee or something. Anywhere. Okay?"

As soon as she'd stepped into his arms, she'd crossed

the line of no return. He understood that and so did she. The realization of what that meant sent a shiver of anticipation rippling through her. What did this man really want from her? And exactly what was she willing to give him? She didn't know the answer to either of those questions. But she was certain of one thing: she wasn't going to run and hide anymore.

"I've not eaten yet," she told him. "Are you hungry?"

"Starved. Let's go get that burger you wanted the other night," he suggested.

"Green Lizard Bar and Grill is just two blocks down from here and it's good. If that's okay with you, I'll follow you in my car," she told him.

"I know where it is." He planted a kiss on her cheek. "I'll wait for you out front."

Moments later, as Lilly drove her car a short distance behind Rafe's truck, she realized her hands were trembling on the steering wheel and she had the strangest sensation of wanting to laugh and cry at the same time.

For years she'd believed she'd lost her ability to feel any sort of desire. She'd thought her chance to experience passion again had walked out the door with Grant. She'd believed her hopes and dreams had died when the baby she'd been carrying was lost to a miscarriage.

But now Rafe had created an explosion inside her. A wonderful explosion that she never wanted to end. The only thing she needed to worry about at this point was keeping her heart separated from the passion. Even if she did throw caution to the wind and go to bed with him, she would never let herself make the mistake of falling in love with him.

## Chapter Four

Green Lizard was an old local establishment with a low-beamed ceiling, planked wooden floor and a long, polished bar equipped with swiveling stools. Behind the counter a bartender was polishing glasses while several customers watched a basketball game on a television hanging on a nearby wall.

As Rafe escorted Lilly to one of the small round tables on the opposite wall from the bar, he wondered if he was one big sap or one of the luckiest men in Nevada. The kiss she'd given him a few minutes ago had been full of promises, but he wasn't sure what those promises had meant, or even if he wanted to be a part of them. He only knew that being with Lilly filled him with a mixture of contradicting emotions. And that was definitely something that Rafe had never experienced with a woman before.

After helping her into one of the wooden chairs, Rafe took a seat directly across from her and reached for one of the single-sheet menus propped between a napkin holder and a tall sugar shaker.

"Since you're ignoring the menu, you must already know what you want to order," he said. "Tell me what's good."

She smiled at him and though it was a genuine expression, he could see the exhaustion in her eyes and around her lips. The thought unexpectedly struck Rafe that he wanted to take her in his arms and soothe away her weariness, to hear her sigh with contentment and see the tension on her lovely face melt away.

"The cheeseburgers are delicious," she told him. "I try to limit myself to one a week, but sometimes I slip and indulge myself with two."

"I'd hardly call that overindulging." He slipped the menu back in place. "Is this where the hospital staff gathers to eat or is it more of a watering hole to relax?"

"A few hit the bar after a long shift. Once in a while I'll have a cocktail, but normally I'm just here for the food. The hospital cafeteria is okay as far as food goes, but after several days of it in a row I need a change of taste."

As soon as Rafe had spotted her walking out of the building tonight, he'd noticed she wasn't wearing her nurse's uniform. Instead, she'd changed into close-fitting jeans and a pink buttoned blouse with sleeves that ended at her elbows. Somehow the casual clothes made her appear even sexier than she had the night they'd dined at the Sierra Chateau. Or maybe it was the softness in her eyes that made her more appealing, Rafe thought. Either way, the sight of her made it very difficult to keep his mind on anything more than kissing her again.

Trying to shake away that tempting image, he asked, "Exactly how long have you worked at Tahoe General?"

"Close to eight years. I was twenty when I first started as an LPN. Three years later, I went back to school and acquired my RN degree."

At that moment a young waitress with a long blond ponytail arrived at their table with two glasses of ice water. After she'd taken their identical orders, Rafe rested his forearms on the tabletop and leaned slightly toward her.

"You look very tired," he told her.

"I'm sorry. It's been a long shift. For the past several hours I've only had a pair of five-minute breaks."

"I wasn't complaining, Lilly. I'm just wondering why you don't work in a clinic? That's meaningful work and the daytime hours would be more normal."

"Yes, it's meaningful. But I think I'd feel trapped." She sipped from the short water glass. "It would be like asking you to keep yourself confined to the ranch yard and never go out on the range."

A wry grin curved one corner of his lips. "I'd feel like a prisoner. I guess when a person is doing something they like the fatigue factor doesn't matter."

"Don't get me wrong, Rafe. A nice, quiet shift is welcomed after an evening like this." With a hand at the back of her neck, she rocked her head from one shoulder to the other. "So tell me about your work. Bart says spring branding is still going on. I can tell he's missing being a part of it."

Rafe grimaced. This was the first spring roundup that Rafe could ever remember his grandfather missing. It was like having breakfast without coffee. It could be done, but it wasn't the same. For years Rafe had wished the old man would allow him to handle things on his own. He didn't need Bart getting in the way or yelling out orders that only tended to get on the crew's nerves. But now that Rafe had gotten his wish, he had to admit that he missed having his grandfather around.

"Yeah. Gramps has never missed roundup. I'm sure it's driving him nuts. He's always been the type to give orders and tell everyone how something should be done. He doesn't think the ranch would survive without him."

Her thoughtful gaze slowly slipped over his face and he wondered what Lilly really saw when she looked at him. Plenty of women had told him he was handsome, but that sort of thing meant nothing to Rafe. Broad shoulders or a strong jaw didn't make a man.

"That's not entirely a bad thing, Rafe. Believing that he's needed is what keeps Bart going. It's pushing him to get well and back on his feet."

"You're probably right about that, but—"

"Probably?" she interrupted. "I am right."

"You're only just now getting to know Bart. He can be demanding, controlling and has a temper that won't quit."

She leveled a meaningful smile at him. "He tells me that you're a lot like him."

He stared at her. "Gramps said that?"

"He did. You seem surprised."

Rafe chuckled. "I've been accused of plenty of things before, but never being like my grandfather. I don't know whether to feel flattered or insulted. Bart is a polarizing figure. You either love or hate him."

"I suspect your feelings for Bart aren't so black or white."

From the very first day he'd met this woman she'd seemed to understand him and he'd immediately known she wasn't the sort he could charm or fool. He respected that about her, yet it jarred him to have anyone, especially a woman, able to read him so easily.

"My feelings for Gramps are hard to define. I love him. But—well, here comes our food. I'll tell you about it later."

The waitress arrived with the cheeseburgers and fries and for the next half hour the two concentrated on eating their meal. Once they'd finished, Rafe paid the ticket and they walked out to the street curb where their vehicles were parked.

"It's still early for me," Lilly said as Rafe escorted her to the door of her car. "Would you like to come by the house for coffee? I made the mistake of going to the supermarket while I was hungry and ended up buying a gallon of rocky-road ice cream. Someone besides me needs to eat it."

Groaning, Rafe patted his midsection. "After all that food, I couldn't eat another bite. But the coffee sounds nice. I'll follow you there."

On the short drive to Lilly's house, Rafe was once again asking himself if he was following her down a dangerous trail or if he should be counting his lucky stars that she was being so warm and inviting.

*You don't have to go to her house, Rafe. If you're that scared of the woman then ring her cell and tell her that something unexpected has come up at the ranch and you're needed there.*

Damn it, he wasn't afraid of the woman. Rafe mentally argued with the voice in his head. He was just a whole lot confused, added to even more caution. The moment he'd first spotted her descending the staircase in his family home, he'd been mesmerized by her. His first thought back then had been to get a date with her. A date that would hopefully lead to a night of incredible sex. But nothing had turned out like he'd planned.

Normally, Rafe would have already dismissed a woman like Lilly from his roster of girlfriends. He didn't have the time or inclination for serious. Now, the fact that he didn't want to cut himself loose from her, that he wanted to court her in an honorable manner, had him mentally shaking his head.

But his confusion wasn't enough to make him steer his truck toward the Silver Horn instead of Lilly's house.

Up until five minutes ago, no man had ever been in Lilly's kitchen. But Rafe had changed all that when he'd insisted on giving her a hand with making the coffee.

Before now, she'd always believed the room had plenty of working space, even with a little pine dining table taking up one whole corner. But Rafe seemed to fill the room. Everywhere she turned or stepped, he seemed to be there with his lazy grin and watchful gaze.

Now, as she stood next to the cabinet counter, waiting for the coffee to finish dripping, she could only wonder what had come over her. Nearly three days ago, she'd called Rafe because she'd been ashamed of her rude behavior. Because she hadn't wanted him to think of her as a shrew or a tease, or a woman who knew nothing about having a relationship with a man. She'd never intended the call to be an invitation. Or had she?

She supposed that question was inconsequential now. With his tall, lean body standing only a step away from hers, she realized more than ever that she'd missed seeing him these past few days. And in the parking lot, when they'd kissed so passionately, she'd felt herself changing. She'd felt herself wanting to give to him. To make him happy and in doing so make herself happy. It was a scary realization. But she was wrapping her mind around it, anyway.

"Looks like this is ready," she said as the coffeemaker gurgled and spit the last few drops. "Would you like to go sit out on the back patio?"

"Sounds nice."

She handed him a mug filled with coffee, then gestured toward a door with paned windows on the top half. "It's out this way."

Lilly's small backyard was shielded from the adjacent neighbors by a wooden privacy fence, while directly at the back a chain-link fence separated her patch of yard from an empty lot shaded by tall cottonwoods and a patch of salt cedars.

After she lit a pair of torches to ward away the mosquitoes, she walked across the red-brick patio to where Rafe had taken a seat on a wooden glider.

As she eased down beside him, Rafe said, "This is nice and quiet. Looks like no one lives directly behind you."

"No. From what I've been told an elderly lady used to live there. After she passed, the old house was torn down. The property passed on to her daughter, but thankfully the woman refuses to sell. Not that I don't like having neighbors. But I enjoy my privacy."

"Hmm. The Horn covers hundreds of thousands of acres and it all belongs to the Calhoun family, but you have to travel far away from the ranch yard to find real privacy. All of my brothers still live at home. And several of our employees, including the resident vet, live not far from the family house. And then there are the single men, who live in the bunkhouse. Someone is always around."

She glanced at him. "Does that bother you?"

He shrugged. "I've never known anything else. Besides, if I want to be alone all I have to do is saddle up and ride in most any direction. The only thing you'll find for miles is cattle, mustangs and other wildlife."

Each time he spoke of the Silver Horn she could hear warm pride in his voice. Clearly, the ranch was the center of his life and she could only wonder if he would ever make room for a woman.

"Rafe, the other day—when I called you—I wasn't expecting this to happen," she admitted.

"When I found your call and drove into town I wasn't expecting to be sitting here with you like this. You haven't exactly been encouraging."

She looked away and across the yard to where a dragonfly fluttered over a birdbath. "That's why I called. I didn't want you to think…well, I didn't want you to take my discouragement personally."

"Lilly, how could I not take it personally?" he asked with comical confusion.

She looked at him and tried to smile, but everything suddenly seemed so complex and serious. She didn't know how to explain herself or if she should even try.

"Like I told you earlier, Rafe, I had a bad experience with a man like you. And since then I've purposely shut myself away."

"A man like me? I'm not sure I like the sound of that."

"Maybe I should have said that differently. This man—he liked women. A lot. And so do you."

The corners of his lips turned downward. "Most men do like women. A lot."

She sighed. "You don't have serious intentions, Rafe. That's what I mean."

"And that makes me villainous?"

She paused for long, thoughtful moments before she finally answered. "I don't think of you in that way anymore. These past few days I realized you were very different from that man I used to know. And I like you. I'm old enough and wise enough now to understand that I can enjoy your company without strings or commitments or any of those things."

He was silent for so long that she was beginning to wonder if she'd offended him somehow, but then he reached over and covered her hand with his.

"I don't suppose you want to tell me about this…man you used to know."

She shrugged one shoulder. "There isn't much to tell. Other than he was a brash, good-looking intern who made me lots of promises he never intended to keep. And I made the foolish mistake of believing him."

"And you've let a man like that scare you away from other men?" He grunted with disbelief. "You must have been wildly in love with the guy."

Had she loved Grant wildly? During their relationship, she'd believed her whole world had hinged on him. She'd believed she'd loved him. But now as the years had wisened her, she was beginning to see that she'd not been in love with Grant; she'd been besotted by him. So much so that she'd been blinded to the reality of their one-sided relationship.

"I was naive and gullible. At that age, I never believed that any man could treat a woman so cruelly." She shook her head. "I got my eyes opened and then later…I supposed I was so soured by the whole ordeal I didn't think any man would be worth the risk of trying to love again. But with you, Rafe, I can see that you're the sort who wouldn't even say the word *love,* much less pretend to harbor that emotion. With you I already know what I'm getting. I don't have to wonder if you're hiding anything."

He placed his coffee mug on the ground then folding his arms against his chest, he shifted in the seat so that he was facing her. The frown on his face said he didn't exactly like her description of him.

"So you think I'm an open book, do you?" he asked.

She breathed deeply, then wondered why it didn't relieve the heavy feeling in her chest. She should be feeling as light as a feather, she thought. She was finally breaking out of her cocoon. And even if nothing could ever come of this relationship with Rafe, it was still a new beginning for her and that was something to feel happy about.

"If a woman ever misunderstands your intentions, it's her own fault," she murmured, then rising to her feet, she walked out to the birdbath, where a patch of wild blackeyed Susans grew around the concrete base.

She was plucking one of the flowers when Rafe walked up behind her and slipped a hand over the top of her shoulder. "I'm not exactly pleased at the image you've painted of me. Coming from you it makes me sound rather heartless. And maybe in lots of ways I am. But I am glad that you're willing to give us a chance, Lilly. We'll have a good time together. And I can promise you one thing. You won't have to worry about me hurting you. I'd never ask you for more than you're willing to give."

She turned to him and as her gaze slipped over his face, it occurred to her that she wasn't worried about Rafe asking her for too much. She was more concerned about herself and the idea that she might end up wanting to give him far more than he wanted. Like a piece of her heart.

But she couldn't allow herself to dwell on that thought now. Starting tonight, she wanted to change the direction of her life. She wanted to be a different woman than the one who'd spent the past five years filling every waking moment with work and very little more.

"I'm not worried. We both understand that we aren't going to get serious. You don't want that and neither do I. We're just going to date. That's all."

For long moments he searched her face. "I agree. But are you sure everything is all right with you?"

"Everything is fine. Why do you ask?"

His fingers gently kneaded her shoulder. "I'm not sure—maybe because you seem different from the Lilly I first met on the staircase."

She smiled at him. "I've needed to be different for a long time, Rafe. And make things in my life better."

Cupping his hand along the side of her face, he smiled back at her and even in the dim glow of the yard lamp, she could see softness in his eyes. The look melted parts of her that had been frozen for far too long.

"I have a feeling everything is going to get better," he murmured. "For me and you. For us."

With that he bent his head to hers and Lilly was only too happy to give him her lips.

The next morning, shortly after nine o'clock, Lilly was about to begin Bart's therapy exercises when he announced he had a surprise for her.

With her hands propped on her hips, she stood in front of his chair. "If you've bought me a gift thinking it will make me soften up on your exercises, then you've wasted your money."

Bart chuckled. "I don't want you to let up on me, Lilly girl. I'd work at this another hour if you'd hang around that much longer."

"Another hour would be too much of a good thing," she told him. "So where is this surprise? Behind your chair?"

"How did you guess?" With a rumbling chuckle, he reached behind the big recliner, but instead of pulling out a sack or box, he was holding a wooden cane with a carved handle.

"Where did that come from? Did your son, Orin, buy it for you?"

Shaking his head, he said, "No. My loving wife gave me this cane years ago when a bull kicked my ankle and broke it. Once I got to walking again, I told her I'd put it away for my golden years. Looks like those years have arrived."

"Nonsense. You're not old yet. You've just had a little setback." She gestured toward the walking stick. "Having said that, I hate to rain on your parade, Bart. You're not ready for a cane. You're still having trouble moving behind a walker."

"The hell you say," he boomed. "Just watch this."

He started to rise from the chair and, expecting him to fall face forward, Lilly automatically lunged toward him and snatched a grip on his arm.

"Bart! Wait! Let me help you!"

With surprising strength, he shook away her hand. "Help be damned! You just get out of the way."

If this had been taking place in the hospital, Lilly would have quickly summoned the help of a strong male nurse, but in this case, she was going to have to deal with Bart's stubbornness herself.

"Bart, if you fall—"

"I'm not stupid. I haven't lost my senses yet."

Realizing the show of independence was, in the long

run, more important than keeping him safely anchored to the chair, she yielded and stepped out of the way.

"All right. If you fall on your ass, I'm not going to feel sorry for you."

Grinning, he slowly but surely straightened to a standing position. "Now you're talking like my kind of woman."

Before she could make any sort of remark to that, he took one shaky step away from the chair and then another until he walked a good ten feet across the room to where a large window gave a vast view of Silver Horn land. When he finally came to a halt, he was out of breath, but the triumph on his face was priceless.

Lilly tried to keep her expression stern as she shook an admonishing finger at him. "You've been getting up and trying to walk without anyone to help, haven't you?"

"I don't want anyone around here pestering me. You're the only one, Lilly, that doesn't get me flustered." His grin was full of pride. "So what do you think of your old man now?"

"I'm very impressed. You keep making this much progress and I won't be needed around here much longer."

His grin swiftly vanished. "If that's the case, I'll start faking it. 'Cause I would surely miss you coming to see me, Lilly."

During her years as a nurse, Lilly had often been told by many patients of how much they appreciated her help and inspiration. But something about Bart growing attached to her was different somehow. Maybe because when she looked at the elder Calhoun, she saw a bit of Rafe.

"You'd better not start faking anything," she warned

him. "When you get totally well, I'll still drive out here to see you from time to time."

"You will?"

She nodded. "Surely. Now come back and sit down so we can begin work on your arm and hand."

More than an hour later, Rafe entered the house by way of the kitchen and found Lilly standing with Greta at the kitchen counter going over a stack of crinkled papers.

She was wearing a white nurse's dress that was nipped in at her tiny waist and stopped just above her knees. Prim white stockings and a pair of low-wedge heels that fastened with a strap across the top of her foot completed her uniform. She managed to look professional and sexy at the same time and just the sight of her was enough to put a spring in his step.

Sweeping off his hat, he ran a hand through his flattened hair as he walked over to the two women.

"Good morning, Lilly. Are you swapping recipes with Greta? She could certainly use a few new ones."

The cook scowled at him. "If you don't like my cooking you can walk straight down to the bunkhouse and eat that hog swill that Percy serves up."

"Shame on you, Greta!" Rafe scolded with a laugh. "Percy is a mighty fine cook. The men tell me he only burns two or three meals a week now. Maybe you ought to go give him some cooking lessons."

Greta batted a hand through the air. "That old man wouldn't listen to a word I told him. Just like a few other men around here that I know," she finished with a pointed look at him.

Rafe tossed a grin at Lilly. "Greta loves me. She'll tell

you that I'm her favorite son. At least, she'll tell you that while my brothers aren't around."

"Don't be lying to the girl. I wouldn't tell you that if we were the last two people on this earth, Rafe Calhoun. You're a scamp. The only thing you're good for is punchin' cows."

Rafe laughed then winked at Lilly. "Greta does a good job at keeping me grounded."

Snorting, the cook gathered up the stack of papers then said to Lilly, "I'll go over these menus with Bart. He'll try to weasel a steak or a dish of ice cream out of me, but don't worry. I'll stick to my guns."

"I'm sure you will, Greta," Lilly told her. "And that's good. But it'll be okay for you to give him a treat once in a while. We want to keep the patient happy."

Greta gave her a conspiring wink. "I'll do my best, Lilly, to make him think I'm letting him get by with something."

The cook left the room and Rafe instantly moved closer to Lilly. "I hadn't expected to see you so soon," he admitted. "We had a pair of flats on one of the horse trailers this morning and had to return to the ranch yard for more tires."

"Five more minutes and I would have been gone," she told him. "I've already finished with your grandfather. But Doctor Kennedy asked me to speak with Greta about Bart's diet."

"Good thing I decided to come to the house and fetch another thermos of coffee." He reached out and wound a tendril of blond hair around his forefinger. "I can tell you how much I enjoyed being with you last night."

Uncertainty flickered in her eyes. "I wasn't sure. You left rather early."

Shortly after the kiss they'd shared in the backyard, he'd told her good-night and driven straight back here to the ranch. A move that had surprised him probably more than it had surprised Lilly.

"You were very tired and you had to be up early this morning." He repeated the same reason he'd given her last night.

But actually, consideration for her work schedule had only been a polite excuse for ending their evening together, Rafe thought. Her kiss had spun him around like a dust devil out of nowhere. If he'd stayed longer, he would have kissed her again. And again. And then he wouldn't have been able to stop with just kissing. Lilly wasn't ready for that. In fact, Rafe wasn't sure if she would ever be ready for that kind of relationship with him. Still, those doubts weren't enough to dampen his desire to be with her.

"I have a short shift today at the hospital. So that helps."

"Short? Then perhaps you'd like to come out for dinner tonight? Greta's cooking Mexican food. And I've been wanting to show you around the ranch. That is, if you'd like to see it."

She shook her head. "I've already promised Bart that he could show me around the place once he's gotten his motor skills back."

Rafe was surprised. Not that she'd promised Bart, but that the old man had invited her on the excursion. His grandfather had always appreciated a pretty woman. But ever since Rafe's grandmother, Gilda, had passed away his grandfather hadn't shown any interest in entertaining one. Until now. Perhaps Bart was falling in love with his nurse? That would definitely put a kink in things, he thought wryly.

"Oh. So my grandfather is competition for me now?" he teased.

She shot him a clever smile. "Bart and I have a special connection. But he's just a tad bit old for me, don't you think?"

Rafe grinned while thinking how much he would like to spend hours with this woman just so he could look at her, hear her voice, drink in her scent and watch the ever-changing expression in her brown eyes.

*Watch it, Rafe, you're getting damned soppy and fast. Before you know it, you'll want to spend days, even weeks with this woman. That's not your style. If you're not careful you're going to be in deep water way before you ever realized you made the jump.*

Blocking out the mocking voice in his head, he answered, "Just a tad. So what about dinner? Can you make it?"

Her little nose wrinkled as she considered his invitation. "I'm not sure, Rafe. Meeting your family might give the wrong idea. Unless you're used to having women over for dinner?"

"I've never invited a woman here to the Horn. But you're different."

Her eyes narrowed with skepticism. "How so?"

He shrugged. "You're Gramps's nurse. You've already made several visits here to the house. It's not like you're a stranger."

She seemed to accept his explanation and Rafe was relieved. He didn't want her getting any ideas. Like she was more special than his past dates. Because she wasn't. She was just like he'd told her—different.

"Okay. I accept." She quickly stepped around him and plucked a tote bag from the end of the cabinet counter. As she walked to the door, she asked, "What time should I be here?"

"Make it six. I should be back to the ranch yard by then."

She gave him a little wave then stepped out the door and Rafe had to fight the urge to race after her and pull her into a tight, passionate embrace.

Yeah, that would be real good, he thought drily. Kissing her like he was about to take his last, dying breath would go a long way in convincing her that he had no intentions of getting serious.

Mentally cursing the thought, Rafe went in search of the coffee thermos and did his best to push Lilly from his mind.

## Chapter Five

Having dinner at the Silver Horn ranch with Rafe was no big deal, Lilly told herself as she drove the last quarter mile up the long drive to the three-story house. She was going to be eating with the same man she'd shared a burger with last night. The only difference tonight would be that some of his family would also be sitting at the table.

Deciding she'd enter the house the same way she did every morning, she parked at the back and headed down a stone pathway that led around the south side of the structure where the kitchen was located.

"Lilly! Wait up!"

At the sound of Rafe's voice, she turned to see him striding across the manicured lawn. As she paused and waited for him to join her, she couldn't help but admire his long-legged stride or the way his white shirt made his features appear even more rugged.

When he reached her side, she said, "I was just going around to the kitchen."

"I was in the family room with Dad and saw you drive up." He wrapped a hand around her arm. "We have a bit of time before dinner will be served. I thought we'd go down to the barns and I'll show you some of the foals born this past month."

"I'd love to," she told him. "I even wore my boots just in case we ventured from the house."

He glanced down at the black, snub-toed boots peeping from beneath the hem of her jeans and smiled. "Very nice. They even have real scuffs on them. I'm impressed."

She smiled smugly. "Nothing drugstore about me, cowboy. I even know how to ride a horse."

"Is that a fact? You couldn't have learned that in nursing school," he said as he urged her into a slow walk across a wide area of hard-packed ground.

She laughed. "No. I learned about riding when I was just a kid. I had a Washoe friend named Blue Jay Bravo. He and his family were our nearest neighbors. His father always had horses and during the summer school break, Blue and I rode everywhere together. Usually bareback and with only a halter for a bridle."

"Hmm. Sounds like you two were little daredevils. I can't imagine you being friends with a little boy."

"Why not? I didn't have any siblings and Blue's two brothers were much older than him and had already left home. It was natural that we became buddies. I was always an outdoor girl, anyway. He was quiet, but when he did say something it was usually very funny and he always made me laugh."

"Where is Blue now or do you know?"

"The last time I spoke with his parents they told me

he lived somewhere outside of Fernley, I think. Training mustangs. He still isn't married. But he should be. He's a great guy. He'd make some woman a nice husband."

"Thank God he lives at Fernley," Rafe said drily. "Otherwise I think I'd be jealous."

Laughing, she cast a droll glance at him. "I doubt you've ever been jealous."

Since Rafe had never had the desire to make any woman his own, he'd avoided feeling jealous or possessive. "Not that I can remember. But there's always a first time."

Wrapping his arm against the back of her waist, he inclined his head toward a group of barns some fifty yards to their right. "Most of the new foals are in a paddock behind the big, red barn. We'll start there first."

Once they reached the structure, Rafe guided her through a maze of gates and alleyways, until they arrived at a tall fence made of wooden boards. Beyond it, a green, grassy paddock stretched over several acres. Inside, broodmares with babies at their sides, nipped at the grass and milled in the flimsy shade of a small stand of desert willows.

While Lilly gazed out at the beautiful animals, she was acutely aware of Rafe standing so close to her that his side was pressing into hers. And though she told herself to move over and put space between them, she couldn't bring herself to break the warm and solid contact. His touch made her feel good. Made her feel protected and wanted. She couldn't give that up. Not yet.

"I've heard that the Silver Horn produced beautiful horses. Now I see why. The babies all look so healthy. I'm not an expert on equine conformation, but to my eye these appear to be top notch."

Rafe gestured out to the foals. "This is stock that will eventually be sold. Our working ranch stock is kept in a different area."

She cast him a thoughtful glance. "If I remember right you said your job was overseeing the care of the cattle. Who oversees the horse management?"

"My younger brother Finn."

"Younger than you? He must be good at his job for Bart and Orin to trust him with such an important division of the ranch."

"Finn is twenty-eight. And he doesn't have complete say-so over things. The final breeding decisions have to be okayed by Dad and Clancy. But otherwise they give him a pretty loose rein."

"I see. And what about you?" she asked curiously. "Do you have complete rein with the cattle and the men?"

Rafe chuckled. "This is a family-operated business, Lilly. Bart isn't going to let any of his grandsons have total control."

As she thought about his response, a little chestnut filly with a blaze face cautiously made her way to the fence where they were standing. Lilly positioned her face between the boards in order to get a closer look at the baby.

"Does that bother you?" she asked Rafe.

After a short pause, he said, "Not really. Sometimes I get aggravated. And there's been plenty of times I've disagreed with a method or decision that I didn't like. But a house divided eventually falls, so I'll always do what's right for the ranch, even if it isn't necessarily right with me personally."

Lilly reached her hand through the fence and the baby tiptoed closer. Just as she was sniffing curiously at her fingers, the mother let out a loud whinny and the filly obediently raced back to the mare's side.

Straightening away from the fence, she looked at him. "I don't suppose you've ever thought about leaving the Silver Horn and setting out on your own?"

"Never. Why? Do you think that's something a man ought to do? Go out on his own? Make his own way?"

She shook her head. "Sometimes. But not in your case. I think it's wonderful that this place means so much to you."

He gazed out at the mares and the thriving babies. "It means everything to me. It's the one thing in my life that I can trust to always be here."

She would've never imagined that a man who changed women as often as he changed shirts would be looking for constancy in his life, but then she supposed she had a lot to learn about Rafe.

"All of your family are here. You can count on them, too," she pointed out.

Even as she said the words, a part of her senses were caught up in his masculine scent, the corded muscles of his forearms resting atop the second rail of the fence, the heat of his body as it pressed against her side.

Since he'd kissed her last night, it was like something inside her had suddenly flared to life. Normally, having sex was the last thing to enter her mind. Now the subject was dominating her every thought.

He said, "Not all my family, Lilly. My mother will never be on this ranch again."

A pang of regret slashed through her and it wasn't only for Rafe's sake that she was feeling the loss. It would be so nice if Claudia was still here. There were so many things Lilly would like to discuss with the woman. She'd been like a mother to Lilly. The kind of mother that Lilly had always wished that Faye would be. But Faye was far too self-absorbed to ever be in the same parenting league as Claudia.

"And you lost a little sister. I'm sure it hurts that she can't be here with all of you."

Slowly, he turned to her and Lilly was amazed to see the incredulous look on his face.

"You knew about Darci?" he asked. "About her dying?"

Why was he so surprised? Lilly wondered. The Calhouns were an old, established family in the area. When a family member died, it was hardly a secret. Then she realized that Rafe was probably thinking Lilly hadn't lived in Carson City long enough to have heard that much about his family. He couldn't know that Claudia had talked to Lilly about losing her little daughter.

"Claudia spoke with me about it when—" she stopped abruptly, then carefully choosing her words, went on "—we became friends at the hospital. I recall her saying her baby had a heart defect that was untreatable."

He nodded ruefully. "That's right. But it's hard to imagine her talking about Darci. Mom kept everything inside and never talked about it to anyone—at least, not that we could see. After Darci died, she stored away all of my sister's things, even the photos that were scattered around the house. It was like she wanted to banish our little sister's existence. I think she and my father quarreled about that, but Mom wouldn't budge."

No wonder Rafe was surprised to hear his mother had confided in her. At the time, Claudia hadn't appeared secretive or reticent when she'd talked about losing her daughter. The woman had been trying to ease Lilly's pain over losing her unborn child by letting her know that she understood because she'd experienced the same sort of grief. But that was something that Lilly was hardly ready to explain to Rafe. In all these years, she'd not told anyone, other than Claudia, about the miscarriage. It was just too painful and private. Moreover, the fact that she'd allowed Grant to get her pregnant only underscored what a fool she'd been to ever trust the man.

"Well, sometimes it's easier to talk about such things to someone outside of the family. And seeing Darci's things was probably just too hard for your mother to deal with. She already had enough images in her heart to remind her of her daughter."

He sighed then eased one arm around her shoulders. "My mom lived among a house full of men. That couldn't have always been easy for her. I'm glad she was able to confide in you. And speaking of confiding, there's something I think I ought to tell you before we go in to dinner—just in case she's brought up."

"*She?* You mean Darci? Or *she* as in one of your girlfriends?"

With a sly chuckle, he urged her away from the fence toward an open doorway of the red barn. "I've never had any long-term girlfriends. So my family can't tell tales on me. I was referring to my sister."

"Oh. Well, don't worry. I won't mention Darci or your mother."

As they continued on a slow path, he cast her a wry glance. "That's not what I'm concerned about. You can mention Mom or Darci anytime that you feel like it."

By now they'd reached the barn entrance. At the left side of the door, a worn wooden bench was pushed up against the outer wall of the building. Rafe gestured for her to join him on the seat.

"Let's set down for a minute."

Even though several ranch hands were tending to evening chores around the barn, none of them were paying special notice to their foreman or his dinner guest. Lilly could only assume that it wasn't unusual for women to visit the ranch. Otherwise, they'd probably be getting a few stares.

After she'd eased down beside him, he said, "Do you remember the other night at the Green Lizard when we were discussing Gramps and I said I'd tell you something later?"

She thought for a moment as she tried to recall their conversation. "I do remember now. But to tell you the truth I'd forgotten it," she admitted. "Why are you bringing Bart up now?"

He grimaced. "Because he's—well, let me start right off by saying that I—that is—my brothers and I have another sister. A living sister."

Her jaw dropped. "A sister! Was she a lot older or something? Claudia never mentioned having another daughter. And Bart has never said anything to me about having a granddaughter."

The frown on his face held a tinge of regret. "Gramps wouldn't. He'd rather forget the whole matter. You see, Sassy is our half-sister."

Lilly's mind began to spin as she tried to keep up with what he was telling her. "Oh. Your dad was married before? I wasn't aware of that, either."

Rafe shook his head. "No. Dad had a brief affair with a woman who used to live in this area. My brothers and I didn't know about Sassy. Dad didn't know about her, either. We found out that she was a Calhoun quite by accident."

Amazed now, Lilly studied him intently. "I'm not sure I'm following you, Rafe. Your father had a brief affair that produced a daughter, but he didn't know about the child until recently?"

Releasing a heavy breath, he raked a hand over his dark hair. "That's right. About a year ago, Sassy traveled out here to Carson City from New Mexico because someone had told her she looked like a Calhoun. She was twenty-four then and looked enough like Finn to pass as his twin."

"That must have shocked everyone—especially Finn. But that hardly proved she was your sister. I guess she had documents or something?"

"No. She was as much in the dark as we were. Then she and Finn decided to do DNA tests. While everyone was waiting for the results to come back, Gramps began acting bizarrely. In fact, he got so worked up he had to be hospitalized. Turns out, he'd been hiding Sassy's existence from Dad and the rest of us. He'd paid off the mother—Marcia Stapleton—to leave town and not tell Orin about the pregnancy. You see, this all happened not long after Darci had died and Mom was in shock with grief. Gramps didn't think Mom could take hearing about her husband having an affair and getting another woman pregnant. Gramps planned to keep tabs on the child and perhaps claim it back into the family once Mom was strong enough to handle the truth. But he lost track of Marcia's whereabouts and whether or not she'd given birth to the child. And Mom—well, I often wonder how she would have viewed Sassy."

"How do the rest of you view her? Does she live around here now?"

Lilly was relieved to see that the smile on his face was full of genuine love. At least the outcome of Sassy's appearance hadn't been all bad, she thought.

"We're all crazy about her. It's great having a sister live close by. She married Jett Sundell about a year ago and they have a baby son. The little tyke is Dad's first grandchild, so he's busy spoiling him."

"I see. Sounds like most everything turned out happily for her and your family. But it shocks me about Bart hiding such information. He seems like such a family man. I can't imagine him keeping something so important from his own son. Orin must have been furious when he found out about Sassy," she mused aloud then looked at him as another thought struck her. "But why didn't this woman go to Orin in the first place? Work things out with him instead of Bart? It doesn't make sense to me."

Rafe shrugged and it was easy for Lilly to see that he wasn't proud of Bart and Orin's past indiscretions. The fact that he was willing to share such intimate family details with her was more than surprising. She'd not expected that from Rafe. Nor had she expected to feel so incredibly drawn to him because of it.

"It didn't make sense to me or my brothers, either. But from what Gramps explains, the woman was more concerned about getting money from the family than she was about her own baby. Dad had already walked away from her—he'd told her flat out that he wanted nothing else to do with her. In her grief Mom had rejected him and he'd turned to this other woman for just a short time. Then he came to his senses. So Marcia must have believed she'd get more money out of Gramps—especially with him being the head of the family and basically hold-ing the strings to the Calhoun fortune. But who really knows. Gramps deceived the family back then. For all we know, he could still be holding back on the way it all really happened."

Feeling more connected to him than ever, she reached over and clasped her hand over his. "I'm glad you shared this with me, Rafe. And I promise, Bart or anyone else won't be hearing anything about this from me."

He squeezed her hand. "I'm not concerned about that. Gramps or Dad might bring up the subject themselves. If they do, at least you'll know the situation." His lips took on a rueful slant. "Now you see why I called Gramps controlling. He's always been that way. But I hope you don't hold any of this against him. I realize you get on well with him and now—"

"Rafe, this isn't going to change my feelings about Bart. We all make mistakes, don't we? And I figure Bart has done a lot of suffering for the choices he made."

He nodded soberly. "So has Dad. But you know what? Having a daughter, no matter the circumstances, has been great for him."

She gave him a gentle smile. "I'm glad to see you've been able to forgive them. You have, haven't you?"

His gaze turned toward the paddock where the mares and fillies were grazing in the falling twilight. "For the most part. Hell, being angry at them won't change what happened. I just—well, I was close to Mom. And when I learned Dad had betrayed her, it sickened me. I often thank God that she never knew. I happen to think the truth would have crushed her."

"Oh, I'm not so sure about that. Claudia was a very wise woman. I'm sure she'd have been hurt, but she also knew she'd not coped with Darci's death well. She was much stronger than you think."

A rueful smile twisted his lips. "You're the first person to ever say that to me. I like to believe you're right."

Rising to his feet, he tugged her up from the bench. "We'd better move on. Greta will have dinner ready soon and before we go back to the house, I'll show you some of the horses that are stabled in the barn."

When Bart had learned that Lilly was coming to dinner, the old man insisted on descending the stairs to join the rest of the family. And though it had taken both Rafe and Orin an exceptionally long time to aid him in getting to the dining room, Lilly could see how much it meant to Bart to be sitting at the head of the table and capable of being in command of his family.

Rafe's youngest brother, Bowie, was away finishing the last of his stint in the Marine Corps. But his other three brothers were present for dinner and each of them greeted her warmly. Clancy, the eldest of the sons was the general manager of the Silver Horn. The tall, tawny-haired man was quiet and reserved, who seemed more content to listen rather than talk. Evan, the detective, was next to Clancy in age, yet different in looks and personality. His intelligent face had a sharp gaze that seemed to be constantly watching and weighing everyone at the table. Then there was redheaded Finn with his wide smiles and buoyant banter. To Lilly, he was more like Rafe than the others and she found herself warmed by his youthful energy.

While they partook of the rich Mexican food, the men generally discussed happenings on the ranch and around the area. Lilly was more than content to simply listen, but everyone around the table was careful to include her into the conversation, which couldn't have been easy since she was the only female.

Once the meal was over, the men excused themselves and scattered in different directions. While Rafe and his father helped Bart back upstairs to his bedroom, Lilly ventured into the backyard where an elaborate set of lawn furniture was grouped near a pair of huge Joshua trees. A star-studded sky stretched endlessly over the desert mountains and as she looked around her, she realized her initial impression of the Silver Horn had changed. It was more than just a rich family's property. The ranch was a home, tatted together by years of hard work and devotion, joys and sorrows.

She was sitting in a cushioned lounger, listening to a sweet medley of night sounds when a hand suddenly dropped onto her shoulder and she looked up to see Rafe standing at the side of her chair.

"Sorry it took so long with Gramps," he apologized. "I think he was tired."

"No doubt. He shouldn't have tried to deal with the stairs. He isn't ready for that. But he's an impatient man."

Rafe chuckled. "Impatient isn't quite the word I'd use. But he was certainly happy about you being here. In fact, he suggested that you stay here on the ranch tonight, since you're only going to drive back here early in the morning. And I agree."

His comment had her swinging her legs to one side of the lounge and sitting straight up. "Stay here? I couldn't possibly do that!"

"Why? We have plenty of empty rooms. Tessa keeps them all fresh and spotless. Just in case we have unexpected guests."

"It's nice of you and Bart to offer, but I'm not pre-pared. A woman needs certain things with her. And—"

He interrupted. "Believe me, we can find anything you need."

She studied the idea for long, thoughtful moments. Staying the night here on the ranch couldn't hurt any-thing, she told herself. After all, it wasn't like she'd be sleeping with Rafe.

"Well, not having to drive back to town tonight and then back out here again in the morning would be nice," she admitted. "Me and my little car would get a rest."

"Now you're talking sense." Grinning happily, he reached for her hand and pulled her from the lounger. "Come on, we'll go in and I'll let you pick out a room."

Once Lilly landed on her feet, she found herself stand-ing so close to Rafe that the front of her body was very nearly pressing into his, and her soft gasp didn't go un-noticed. Before she could step aside and move away from the temptation, his arms slid around her and with his hands splayed at the back of her waist, he urged her closer until she was clamped against him.

"Rafe! We're out here in the wide open. Your family might see us!"

The grin on his face deepened. "It's dark out here, Lilly. And I really doubt any of them are looking. Be-sides, we're not doing anything scandalous."

"Bart warned me that you were naughty," she said. "Now I see why."

"Naughty or nice—all I could think about during din-ner was having you in my arms like this."

"Hmm. I thought the only thing on your mind was the food."

He rubbed his knuckles beneath her chin. "And I got

the impression that my brothers were the only thing on your mind."

She chuckled slyly. "Coming from a man who says he never gets jealous, that's an odd statement."

"There's a first time for everything," he said gruffly, then bending his head, he settled his lips over hers.

Something was different. The search he was making of her lips was more than a kiss. It was more like a man burning his brand on one of his possessions. Even as she was being swept along in his dark, masculine taste, the thought was zinging through her head, warning her that things between them were changing and evolving at an all too rapid rate.

Yet she was helpless to stop it. And why would she want to? Being with Rafe made her feel needed and wanted. He made her feel like a woman again. And no matter what happened in the future, she deserved to let herself have that much in life. Didn't she?

## Chapter Six

When Rafe finally ended the kiss, Lilly's hands were clenching the sides of his waist in order to keep herself upright, while her lungs labored to regain her breath.

"I could get used to this," he murmured as he rested his cheek against the top of her head.

She licked her lips and realized they were partially numb as a result of his ardor. "Are you talking about the kiss? Or me being here on the ranch?"

"Both."

Not wanting to follow the serious direction of his remark, she said on a teasing note, "After a bit you'd get bored with both."

Lifting his head, he studied her for long moments and Lilly wished she could see the thoughts behind his gray eyes.

"Would I?" he asked softly.

She did her best to let out a light laugh, even though

she wasn't feeling the least bit humorous. "Pie is delicious. But eating it every day might ruin the specialness."

He chuckled suggestively. "Not with my sweet tooth."

With an arm at the back of her waist, they strolled to the house and entered the structure through a door that led them down a hallway toward the family room. Along the way, they spotted Tessa carrying a tray of coffee and cookies toward the staircase landing.

Rafe immediately signaled to the young woman wearing a black dress uniform with a brown bun fastened to the back of her head.

"You need something, Rafe?" she asked.

He smiled at the young maid. "Ms. Lockett is going to be spending the night with us. Do you have the green room tidied up?"

"I do. And as far as I know there aren't any guests scheduled to be arriving anytime soon."

"Well, I told Lilly she could choose the room she wanted, but I think she'd like the green room."

The maid cast Lilly a sly, curious glance then shifted it back to Rafe. "I'm sure of it."

Lilly looked at Rafe. "Any place with a bed will do fine for me."

"Lilly doesn't have any personal, overnight things with her," Rafe explained to the maid, "so she might need for you to round up—uh—whatever it is you women need at night."

Tessa nodded at Lilly. "Just punch the in-house button on the telephone, Ms. Lockett. I'll be glad to get whatever you need."

A maid at her disposal. Lilly had never lived in such an opulent manner. In fact, she'd never even dreamed of working in a home like this, much less spending the night as a guest. The realization pointed out the stark differences between her and Rafe. Yet at the same time, she truly believed that Rafe wasn't defined by his wealth. If he had been, he'd never have taken a second glance at her. And she definitely wouldn't be standing here by his side.

"Thanks, Tessa."

With a smile and nod, the maid continued on up the staircase while Rafe gestured toward a wide hallway that led to another wing of rooms on the ground floor.

As they walked along, he said, "My brothers, Dad and Gramps all have bedrooms upstairs. I'm the only one who stays here on the ground floor."

"Why is that? You just want to be different?" she asked him.

He chuckled. "No. It's more out of convenience. During calving season, I often have to leave the house in the middle of the night. It's easier not to have to fumble my way down a flight of stairs."

At the end of the hallway, he stopped at a door to their right, opened it and reached around the facing to switch on the light. "Here it is. Look around and see if it suits you."

Pausing at the threshold, she asked, "Where is your room?"

Grinning cleverly, he pointed back in the direction from where they'd come. "Way down there at the opposite end of the hallway. Worried I might sleepwalk?"

Blushing, she stepped into the bedroom. "No. Just curious."

Trying to push away the tantalizing image of Rafe lying in bed, she stepped farther into the room then went stock-still as she stared incredulously at her surroundings.

Other than a massive four-poster bed with a matching

cherrywood chest and dresser, there was also a sitting area furnished with a long couch, a love seat, a writing desk, a small bookcase filled with hardbound books and an entertainment center supplied with a television, DVD player and stereo system.

The walls were painted a soft, celery-green while the bedcovers and drapes were a deep, emerald color. Except for a white-and-green Berber rug positioned at the side of the bed, the floor was all varnished hardwood.

She looked at him and shook her head. "I said all I needed was a bed, Rafe. This is a suite!"

Ignoring her protest, he walked over to a wall of drapes and began to pull them to one side. "Come here and look. When you wake up in the morning you can see the mountains. So you can have coffee in bed or here on the love seat. Or you can sit out on the small terrace and watch the horses play."

First he'd invited her to a family dinner and now this. They'd both agreed they weren't going to get serious, but this certainly seemed more than casual. But then she was probably making too much of things, she told herself.

With a short, disbelieving laugh, she walked over to where he stood by the sliding glass doors. "You make it sound like I'm a lady of leisure. I wouldn't know what it's like to have coffee in bed."

"We need to do something about that," he said with a sly grin then taking her by the hand, he led her over to the couch. "Let's sit. I want to hear what you thought of my brothers."

Pulling her down beside him, he quickly wrapped his arm around her shoulders and cuddled her close to his side. Lilly was instantly consumed by the warmth of his body and an overwhelming sense of protection. Which didn't make sense. No one had to tell her that being this near to Rafe was dangerous. Yet something about his touch made her feel safe and special.

"Your brothers? Well, all three were nice, mannerly and interesting. I liked them all."

He groaned. "That was a polite, automatic response. Tell me what you really thought."

"Well, Clancy seems very reserved and more serious than the rest of you."

"That's true. Clancy keeps his feelings pretty much to himself. He's all business."

"Did he fall into the job of managing the ranch because he's the eldest? Or is that something he always wanted to do?"

"Hmm. I don't think Clancy's age has anything to do with him becoming manager. He's more qualified. He has a college degree in ranch management. Finn and I have some college under our belts, but the two of us are mainly just good cowboys."

"In other words, you and Finn have plenty of hands-on training," she said.

"Plenty." He shifted around on the cushion so that he was facing her. "It probably seems to you like we were born into luxury. And I guess we were in many ways, but Dad or Gramps have never just handed things out to me or my brothers. From the time we were old enough to lift a rake or carry a feed bucket we've had to work. Whether that was mucking stalls or feeding calves or sweeping the tack-room floor, we've had to do our part."

"You should be glad they taught you that work ethic," she said. "But I'm curious about Evan and Bowie. What did your parents think about them working outside of the ranch? I have the feeling that Bart didn't approve."

Rafe shrugged. "He doesn't approve. But we are different men, Lilly. Evan has always liked ranching and to be honest, he's very good at it. But he felt a calling for the law. And I admire him for sticking to his dream and becoming a deputy sheriff. Even though he did catch plenty of hell for it. Besides signing away his part of the annual profit from the ranch."

"Wow. That was a steep price to pay—just to do something he loved," Lilly said with a shake of her head. "And Bowie? I take it he must be strong minded, too."

Rafe chuckled. "Our youngest brother has always had a wild streak. Not in a mean way, though. Just adventurous. He caught plenty of flak from Dad and Gramps when he signed up with the Marine Corps. But both admit that the years Bowie spent in the military honed him into a stronger man."

She sighed. "I can't imagine how it must feel to have so many siblings. I always wanted brothers and sisters. But it never happened. My parents—" she hesitated, then dropping her gaze to her lap, went on in a rueful voice "—they were always too busy fighting to ever have more children."

"Am I wrong or didn't you tell me that your parents are still together?"

"They are still living together. But that's about the extent of it. Mom is the type who's never satisfied. And Dad is—well, he tries not to take things too seriously. That only infuriates Mom even more. When I see what they've done to each other it's easy for me to swear off marriage."

"And have you? Sworn off marriage, I mean."

She'd not expected him to ask such a personal, point-blank question. She couldn't imagine him being interested one way or the other about her thoughts on marriage. He probably wanted to be reassured that she wasn't really hunting for a husband.

"When I was younger I used to dream about getting married. I'm not anything like my mother so I'd always believed things would be different for me. There would be no fighting or hurting or tears. But then I learned that kind of thinking was just a fairy tale and I decided I didn't want any more pain or tears than I'd already endured."

His gray gaze was solemn as he studied her face. "What about children? You're a nurse. You're bound to have a nurturing, maternal instinct. A desire to have a baby."

The mere word had her throat constricting with emotions. Forgoing men for the past few years had been easy. Putting aside the dreams of having a baby had been very hard. "I won't lie to you, Rafe. I'd like to have children. But I'm an old-fashioned type of woman. I happen to think children need a father, too. And that would require a husband. So…I've put the whole idea away." Blinking at the tears stinging the backs of her eyes, she looked up at him. "Why are you asking me this, anyway?"

He glanced away and Lilly got the feeling that he'd already regretted his questions.

"I don't know, exactly. I suppose because we were talking about my brothers and our families." His gaze returned to her face. "And I guess the more I get to know you, the more I wonder why a lovely woman like you is living alone—without any attachments."

Uncomfortable now, she rose from the couch and wandered aimlessly over to the window. With the drapes pulled open, a twinkle of yard lamps spread across the ranch yard and cast dim pools of light over parts of the broodmare pasture where she'd watched the foals play. No doubt, in the light of day it would be a beautiful sight. But the more she looked around her, the more she realized that Rafe was only a temporary pleasure in her life. In a matter of time he would move on to some other woman and she'd have to be ready to deal with that reality.

"Rafe, I've told you—"

"Yeah. You've told me about the intern. I haven't forgotten. But—" Suddenly, he stopped and shook his head. "Never mind. We don't need to be spoiling our evening talking about this kind of stuff."

She sighed with relief. "I completely agree."

Grinning now, he walked over to where she stood and slipped his arms lightly around her waist. "What do you say we go upstairs and have some coffee with Dad? I know he'd enjoy your company. Since Mom died I think he gets lonely."

For a man who was rumored to be a self-absorbed playboy he wasn't exactly behaving like one. This wasn't the first time she'd noticed him considering the feelings of others before his own and the notion endeared her more than he could ever know.

"I'd love to have coffee with your father."

"Great. And if you're worried about consuming caffeine at this hour of the evening, Greta will make you a pot of decaffeinated."

She laughed. "Rafe, I often work the night shift. I'm used to drinking coffee at all hours of the day or night."

With a sly little grin, he urged her toward the door. "Then I won't feel a bit guilty about keeping you up late tonight."

\* \* \*

Two days later, Rafe was tossing several lariats and branding irons into the bed of his truck when he heard a footstep behind him.

Glancing over his shoulder, he spotted Denver, his ramrod, sauntering up and from the grim look on the man's face, he clearly wasn't happy about something.

Turning, Rafe cut straight to the matter. "What's wrong?"

"Selby's mare, Opal, has come up lame this morning. Doc doesn't think it's serious, but she's going to have to be turned out to pasture for at least three months before we can use her again. Selby needs a mount and all that's left in the pen this morning is Lute. He's—"

Rafe interrupted with a shake of his head. "A bit of an idiot if something comes along to spook him. I don't want Selby on him today. We've got mountain riding to do. Tell him to—" He stopped and thought a moment. "Just wait until I get to the saddling paddock."

"What about the rest of us?" Denver asked. "You want us to load up and head on out?"

"What part of that did you not hear? I said wait! We'll all leave together!"

From the look on the ramrod's face, Rafe could see he hadn't appreciated his gruff reply.

Heaving out a heavy breath, he wiped a hand over his face. "Sorry, Denver. I didn't mean to be so short. I'm just getting damned tired of being without enough horses."

"It is getting to be a problem," Denver agreed. "We've had a rash of mounts come up either sick or injured. And some of them have just been overworked during this roundup. Finn needs to—"

"Wake up!" Rafe finished hotly. "I'll be at the paddock in a few minutes."

Turning on his heel he started toward the broodmare barn, his long, angry strides eating up the ground.

When he entered the building he had serious doubts he'd find his brother there. Finn had an annoying habit of being anywhere other than where he was supposed to be. But to Rafe's surprise, he found his younger brother about to step into a small office situated in between a row of horse stalls.

The moment he spotted Rafe's approach, he paused at the threshold and waited until he was within earshot before he spoke.

"Rafe, what are you doing here? I thought you and the guys were leaving for the White Pine range this morning?"

"That was the plan! We should have been gone thirty minutes ago!"

"So why are you hanging around here? Did someone tell you that I needed to see you?"

"Hell, no! I need to see you! For the past two weeks I've been trying to corner you, but you're always gone or busy. This can't wait any longer!"

Finn's jaw tightened. "What are you talking about? You've had all kinds of opportunities to talk with me. We were sitting together at the dinner table two nights ago!" he shot back at him.

Rafe clenched his teeth together as he tried to hold on to his patience. "You expect me to discuss business in front of Lilly?"

"Aw, yes, Lilly," Finn drawled in a suggestive tone. "I'm still trying to figure out what you're doing with her."

"What the hell is that supposed to mean?"

Finn stepped through the office door and motioned for Rafe to join him. Once both men were inside the small room, Finn shut the door.

"Are you trying to insult Lilly? Because if you are you're begging to get your head knocked off," Rafe warned him.

Unperturbed by Rafe's show of temper, Finn shook his head and sank into a chair behind a desk piled with papers and empty coffee cups. "Don't be stupid. Lilly is a nice woman. A very nice woman. That's why I'm asking what you're doing with her. She's not your style."

"And how do you know what my style is?" He flung the question at Finn.

His brother shrugged. "Think about it, Rafe. You'll figure it out—eventually."

Deciding not to let this encounter turn into something about Lilly, Rafe said, "I didn't come down here to the barn to discuss my personal life with you, Finn." Shoving one corner of the desk free of clutter, Rafe eased a hip onto the space. "I'm here to talk to you about the remuda. Or I should say—the lack of one. Spring roundup has worn out the whole string. We've not had enough mounts to rotate this past week. And this morning Selby's mare has come up lame. Lute is the only animal left in the remuda and he's not worth a damn in the mountains."

"I know all about Opal turning up lame," Finn cut in. "Doc says it's a soft-tissue injury. She'll have to be put to pasture for at least three months before she's ridden again."

Rafe stared at him. "You knew about this? Damn it, why didn't you call me?"

Finn's indifferent expression made Rafe want to curse a blue streak.

"What good would that have done?" Finn countered. "Denver or Selby would've explained everything to you."

Rafe's teeth ground together. "Denver or Selby doesn't manage the Horn's horses. And apparently, you don't, either!"

Finn frowned at him. "Why are you here trying to jump down my throat and pick a fight with me? I've been doing my job."

"Like hell! All you've done for the past three months is moon over those mares and colts. Well, let me tell you, brother, there's more to this ranch than breeding and selling horses! How do you expect me and my men to work cattle without mounts?"

"Rafe, finding dependable working horses isn't that easy. I don't have to tell you that. I'm trying to locate some now, but I'm not going to drive all over the country picking up one here and two or three over there. I'm in the middle of making a deal for twelve from the Sandbur down in Texas. If that goes through, they'll ship them to us."

Rafe rolled his eyes toward the ceiling. "And when might that be?"

"I can't say. A deal like this can't be pushed," he said, then seeing Rafe's disgust, he went on, "Look, brother, I'm trying to save the ranch some money by making a few negotiations. You ought to understand that."

"What I understand is that the ranch is losing money if cattle go unfound and uncared for. Think about that, Finn. Or does that even matter to you?"

Rafe didn't wait around to hear Finn's response. The men were waiting on him. Besides, he'd made his point. There wasn't any use in continuing to argue his case.

At the end of the barn, he stepped out the same door

that he and Lilly had walked through the evening she'd come to dinner. From the corner of his eye, he caught a glimpse of the bench where the two of them had talked, and the sight caused him to pause and wipe a cleansing hand over his face.

He'd not seen Lilly since he'd told her good-night and she'd retired to the green room, and that had been two nights ago. With his schedule being packed and punctuated with minor emergencies, and her shifts at the hospital ever changing, he'd not had the chance to see her and had only talked to her once when she'd called to thank him for dinner. And even that contact had been cut short with a problem on the ranch that needed his immediate attention.

Not being with Lilly was doing something to him, Rafe realized. Not being able to see her, talk to her and touch her was like eating a huge meal and still feeling hungry. No matter what he ate, the gnawing pains remained. And that troubled him greatly.

The woman was getting some sort of hold on him and to make matters worse, she wasn't even trying.

*I'm still trying to figure out what you're doing with her.*

Finn's remark had cut deep. Not because he was annoyed with his younger brother over the horse situation. But mostly because Rafe had been wondering the very same thing. Lilly wasn't his sort of woman. In spite of what she'd told him about love and marriage and babies, she was the type who needed all three. And Rafe wasn't about any of those things. Not since his mother had died and he'd watched his father's grief turn him into a shadow of the man he'd once been.

Yet everything he'd been doing with the woman said

otherwise. But in all truth, he'd never planned on inviting Lilly to a family dinner or sharing private details of their lives with her. Whenever he was with her, things just seemed to roll out of his mouth of their own volition. He'd never entertained the idea of asking her to stay the night on the Horn, either, but somehow that had happened, too, thanks in part to his grandfather.

And even though Rafe had done nothing more that night than give her a chaste good-night kiss outside the door of the green room, he'd gone to his own room and lain awake for hours, aching to make love to the woman. He was still aching.

No. That wasn't Rafe's style. He'd never let any woman make him this needy before. So what was he going to do about it? About her?

The sudden ring of his cell phone jarred Rafe out of his thoughts and reminded him that he'd wasted too much time staring at a bench and thinking about a woman.

Taking off in long, frustrated strides toward the saddling paddock, he jammed the phone to his ear. "Yeah, Denver. I'm coming," he said to the ramrod. "Get the horses loaded. Lute, too."

"Start an IV on this patient now, Nurse. He's going to surgery."

Not trusting that she'd heard the doctor correctly, Lilly looked around at him. "Surgery? But Doctor, he's not gone to X-ray yet. He might—"

The young doctor stalked over to where she was drawing pain medicine into a small syringe and studied the name tag pinned to her uniform.

"I don't think I need to remind you, Lilly, that I'm the

doctor here. You are the nurse. You follow my orders," he said briskly.

*And you can kiss my—you know what,* she thought, as she shot him a challenging stare. The doctor had only come to work at Tahoe General a few months ago and during that time he'd made far more enemies than friends among the nursing staff. Lilly had tried her best to get along with him, but she couldn't stand by and let him bypass proper procedures.

A few steps away, the middle-aged patient lying on an examining table spoke, "Nurse Lilly is right. I ain't going to no surgery."

Stabbing Lilly with another glare, the doctor returned to the patient's side. "Trust me, Mr. Vaughn, your ankle is broken. The surgeon will want to take X-rays of his own before you go into surgery. There's no point in making two sets."

"Like hell! I twisted my ankle. I didn't come here for a knife-carving party. All I wanted was something to kill the pain." Throwing his legs over the side of the bed, he motioned for Lilly to hand him his pants then added with disgust, "I'm outta here!"

For the next few minutes an argument ensued with Doctor Sherman insisting that the patient couldn't leave, but in the end he couldn't stop the man from hobbling out of the examining room, then signing a release form and walking out of the hospital.

By the time the whole scene had ended, Lilly was already tending to another female patient with a head wound that was bleeding profusely. But rather than deal with the half-hysterical woman, the doctor ordered Lilly to join him out in the hallway.

"I think you ought to know that I'm reporting this

whole incident to the director of nursing. He'll deal with you accordingly."

Lilly's chin lifted. "For trying to follow the correct procedure? I hope you do report it to Mr. Anderson."

His expression turned malicious. "You and I both know the man's ankle was broken. You were deliberately trying to usurp my position in front of the patient."

If she allowed it, Lilly's temper could be just as explosive as her mother's. And there was nothing she'd like better at this moment than to tell this ego-bloated doctor what she thought of him. But through the years she'd trained herself to remain calm, even when she was under fire.

"Mr. Vaughn didn't know it. And neither did I. Unlike you, I needed to see an X-ray to determine that. Now if you'll excuse me, there's a patient in there losing a lot of blood."

Later that evening as Lilly drove home, she wondered if her wretched day was ever going to take a turn for the better. Her day had been long, to say the least, and in spite of the run-in with Doctor Sherman, and her mother ringing her cell for the past two hours, her thoughts remained steadfastly stuck on Rafe.

Slowly and surely the man had become an important fixture in her life. It was becoming unbearable to go a day without seeing him, touching him. What did it mean? Moreover, what was she going to do about it?

As she stepped into the house and the landline began to ring, Lilly was forced to put the questions about Rafe aside and pick up the phone. Otherwise, her mother would continue to call both phones until she answered.

"Hello, Mom."

"Lilly! I was beginning to wonder if you were still alive!"

Lilly didn't bother to hide her sigh as she kicked off her shoes and pulled the bobby pins from her bun. "Mom, you know I can't be talking on the phone while I'm at work. And the E.R. has been swamped. I've just now walked into the house."

"Well, that doesn't mean you can't take two minutes to send me a text! I've been going through a living hell these past two days."

A living hell for Faye was a bad hair day or missing an episode of her favorite television program. Dealing with a real problem usually sent her to bed with a headache. "I've not exactly been on a vacation myself, Mom."

Faye snorted. "You don't have a husband telling you what you can or can't do! Just because I bought a new couch for the den, your father is having a fit. He's still threatening to make me send it back. And I'm not about to do that. It's too embarrassing!"

Carrying the cordless phone toward the kitchen, Lilly tried to reason. "Dad probably thinks you can't afford the piece of furniture."

Faye muttered an expletive. "Every time I say we need something, he starts whining about saving for retirement. What are we supposed to do now? Live like paupers?"

The splitting pain in Lilly's forehead was worsening with each word her mother spoke and instead of pulling a cold soda from the fridge, she opened a cabinet and reached for a bottle of aspirin.

"Look, Mom, I just got home. I need to change out of my uniform and—"

"Sure, cut me off. You're just like Ron. I don't—"

In the midst of her mother's prattle, Lilly heard a

knock at the door and was actually relieved for the distraction. At this point dealing with a pushy salesman would be better than Faye's complaining.

"Sorry, Mom. Someone is at the door. I'll have to call you later."

Always careful to check through the peephole before opening the door, Lilly was totally surprised to see Rafe standing on the small porch. His faded jeans and white shirt looked as though he'd come straight from the cattle pen and the fearful thought that an emergency had occurred on the Silver Horn had her fumbling to open the door.

"Rafe! What are you doing here? Is anything wrong?"

"No." Pulling the crumpled straw cowboy hat from his head, he gestured toward the doorway. "May I come in?"

More than flustered, she raked a hand through her tousled hair. "Oh. Of course. Please do."

She stepped aside to allow him to enter and while he walked to the middle of the room, she dealt with closing and locking the door behind her.

"I'm sorry, Lilly. I shouldn't have just showed up like this. I'm still in my dirty work clothes and you weren't expecting me."

Dirty or not, the mere sight of him was filling her with joy. "None of that matters."

"I tried calling, but all I could get was your voice mail."

"I'm sorry. I should have explained to you that during work I have to keep my phone turned off. I've just now gotten home from the hospital. But I'm glad you're here."

"Are you?"

She meant to cross the floor slowly, to remain cool and collected and not let him see how much she'd missed him.

But her intentions couldn't overpower the need to be close to him. Rushing the last few steps to him, she flung her arms around him and nestled her cheek against his chest.

"I've missed you, Rafe. Very much."

Even before she'd finished speaking, his arms were wrapping around her, drawing her close.

"And I've missed you, Lilly. I didn't want to go another day without seeing you. So I drove into town in hopes of finding you home."

Tilting her head back, she looked up at his face. "My day has been horrible. Seeing you—oh, I'm so glad you're here, Rafe."

"Ever since that night you stayed at the ranch I haven't been able to think of anything but you." Cradling her head with his hands, he lowered his face to hers. "When I kissed you good-night outside the door of the green room I didn't want to leave. I wanted to take you inside and make love to you."

Just hearing him say the words was enough to infuse her whole body with heat. "I was awake for a long time that night—wondering if you might come to me. And wondering what I'd do if you did come."

His gray eyes were serious as they probed hers. "And if I had? What would you have done?"

Something inside her suddenly crumbled, and she realized she could no longer hide from the things he was making her feel and want.

"I would have welcomed you into my bed."

He didn't utter a word. Instead, his mouth swooped down on hers and for the next few moments he kissed her so deeply that Lilly could feel her senses slipping away, her legs turning to useless mush.

When their lips finally parted, Lilly's heart was

pounding out of control and her hands were gripping the front of his shirt. She'd never felt so aroused in her life, so drunk with desire.

"I want you so much, Lilly," he whispered against the side of her neck. "From the first moment I saw you I wanted you. Like this. And this."

As his lips made a slow, wet trail down the side of her neck, his fingers worked loose the buttons on the upper part of her dress and he pushed the fabric off her shoulder as his mouth continued its blistering descent.

With each touch of his hand, each caress of his lips, Lilly felt her body yielding, molding to whatever he wanted it to be. Yet she'd never felt so alive, so acutely aware of every sound and scent, every throbbing ache building deep in the core of her.

"My legs," she finally managed to whisper. "I can't keep standing."

"And I don't want to," he agreed, then sweeping her up in his arms, he asked, "The couch?"

Now was the moment, she thought. Either give all of herself to this man, or close herself off and wonder for the rest of her life what might have been.

Curling her arms around his neck, she whispered, "My bedroom. Behind you to the right."

## Chapter Seven

Lilly's bedroom was cool and the faint scent of tropical flowers lingered in the air. The shades were pulled down and, except for a shaft of light filtering through the doorway, the room was mostly dark. Rafe managed to see the outline of a queen-size bed and he placed Lilly in the center of the mattress then stretched out alongside her.

She reached for him at the same time his arm curled around her waist and as he tucked her head beneath his chin, he whispered close to her ear, "I never expected to be here like this. But you have a habit of making me do the unexpected."

Tilting her head, she planted a kiss on his chin and then another on his jaw, and the simple sweetness of her response was unlike anything he'd ever experienced before. And for long moments all he could do was hold her close, breathe in the scent of her hair and let the warmth of her body seep into his.

"I wasn't exactly planning on this happening tonight, either," she replied in a low, husky voice. "But I knew it was coming soon. Neither one of us could stop it."

Stop it? He'd thought all along he'd been working toward this very moment. But perhaps subconsciously he'd been trying to hold back. Because he'd known that this thing with Lilly would be different. And he feared it as much as he wanted it.

Groaning at the thought, he began to plant kisses over her forehead. "That would be like trying to stop the rain or the wind. Impossible."

Her hand cupped the side of his face and urged his lips toward hers. Rafe was more than glad to surrender, and in a matter of seconds the meeting of their mouths turned into a frenzied feast, each of them searching for more and more. And even though Rafe kept telling himself to slow down and take his time to touch and savor each exquisite curve of her body, the desire erupting inside him had his hands and mouth moving in a blind rush.

Ripping his mouth from hers, he finished with the last buttons on her nurse's dress, then folded back both sides of the fabric to reveal a full white slip edged at the neckline and hem with delicate ecru lace.

Easing back on his feet, he studied her in the dim light. "Wow! I thought women quit dressing like this back in the 1960s!"

Under the circumstances, the prim press of her lips seemed ridiculously funny. But he couldn't laugh. Not when the sight of her was virtually taking his breath away.

"Sorry to disappoint you, Rafe, but some of us still dress like ladies."

"Disappoint? Lilly, you're the sexiest woman I've ever seen in my life. Sexy, beautiful, delicious."

As he said the last word, he planted hands on either side of her waist and bent his head to the valley between her breasts. The feel of her skin against his tongue was incredibly soft and tasted like sweet cream. Like a hungry cat, he wanted to lap it all up then search for more.

Unfortunately, the beautiful slip and white lace bra beneath it became an irritating barrier and after a few moments, he shoved the hem upward to her armpits.

Sensing his need, she rose to a sitting position and held up her arms so that he could ease the garment over her head. Once it and her bra were out of the way, his hands cupped both small breasts as he dipped his head and laved each pink nipple with his tongue.

In the silence of the room, he could hear each ragged intake of her breath and each time his mouth moved to a new spot, her breathing grew faster and faster while her fingers dug into his hair and clung to his scalp.

Eventually, her lower body began to writhe against his and she pushed his mouth away from her breasts and gasped.

"Rafe—please—love me now! This second!"

The urgency in her thick voice washed him with waves of heat. Feeling as though he was about to explode, he hurriedly began to tug off his boots and clothing. All the while, he could feel her gaze upon him, watching, waiting and weighing.

When he finally stepped out of his boxers, he felt ridiculously exposed and for the first time in his life, he wanted a woman to look at him and want him. Not because he was a wealthy Calhoun or because he had a long, lean, muscled body that could give her pleasure, but because of all the things she could see inside him. The needs and wishes, the disappointments and pains.

"I have protection in my wallet. If you—"

Before he could finish, she interrupted, "I'm already protected with oral birth control. But if you're worried—"

He arched a brow at her. "The pill?"

Her mouth curved with wry assumption. "You're thinking I'm promiscuous now."

His low chuckle was nothing about humor. Instead, it held a wealth of affection.

"Oh, Lilly, baby. I'm thinking nothing of the sort. I'm thinking—" Leaning over her, he brushed back a tendril of hair dangling close to her eye. "To be honest I—I've never been that bare with any woman before. And the idea—"

He stopped, unsure of how to go on, or even if he should.

"Scares you," she finished for him.

He traced his forefinger along her cheekbone and down her pert little nose. "Maybe. But not nearly as much as it excites me. When I'm inside of you I'll be able to feel you—all of you against me."

His throat was so thick he could barely get the last word out. But by then it didn't matter as her hand curved around the back of his neck and tugged his mouth down to hers.

The contact drew him onto the bed with her and as their naked bodies intertwined and their tongues danced together, he was assaulted with so many sensations he was suddenly drunk. Everything around him was blurring, whirling to a place where she was the anchor and without her he'd float off into velvety darkness.

Somewhere among his splintered awareness, he could

feel her small hands skimming over his back and shoulders, down his arms and over each bump of his ribs. At the same time, his hands were racing over each curve, every dip and valley of her body, while his own body was screaming at him to make the final connection.

When his hand slipped between her soft thighs and his finger found the moist folds, she groaned deep in her throat, and in that moment he thought he would split apart.

Lifting his head, he looked down at her. "Lilly, is this really what you want? Tell me. Tell me now or—"

Her hands came up to frame his face. "Rafe, I want you. All of you," she whispered.

If there'd been an ounce of hesitancy in her voice he would've somehow found the willpower to pull away from her. But he heard no doubts and the notion that she trusted him to this extent caused his chest to swell with inexplicable emotions.

"And I want all of you, Lilly."

Her legs parted and her hands latched on to his shoulders. With his eyes on her shadowed face, he shifted his hips over hers and slowly entered. As her body accepted him, surrounded him with moist heat, he momentarily lost his breath and his teeth snapped together as he fought to hang on to his control.

Before he could fill his lungs with air, her hips were already thrusting upward, drawing him deeper inside, and he had no choice but to follow her needy movements. And suddenly, thinking had nothing to do with it. Everything was about feeling, touching and tasting.

Faster and faster, their bodies melded together and moved as one as they raced toward the spot where relief would engulf them and toss them higher than the star-studded sky.

Somewhere along the way Rafe recognized that he was lost and that this was a journey he'd never taken before, but it was too late to be afraid and far too late to turn back.

With his mouth devouring hers, he mindlessly drove himself into her. Over and over. Until there was nothing left in him. Nothing to stop him from stepping over the edge. And as his seed spilled into her, something else went with it, something that felt oddly like his heart.

For long, incredible moments Rafe felt like an empty vessel, free-falling, drifting aimlessly through a cloud of magical stardust. Until finally, he realized his face was buried between her breasts and her fingers were sliding through his damp hair.

"You have beautiful hair. Did you know that?"

Her remark was so sweet and unexpected, he tried to chuckle, but the sound came out more like a weary gasp.

"All of that and the woman is fixated on my hair," he teased. "Surely, there was a little more than my hair that impressed you."

Groaning, she pushed him onto his back then draping her upper body over his, she pressed the pad of her forefinger to the middle of his chin. "I'm impressed with every bit of you, Rafe Calhoun."

Her face was bathed in the soft light filtering through the doorway and he was amazed at how familiar and precious her features had become to him. No matter what happened from this night forward, the image of her like this, with a sheen of sweat on her face and her golden hair tousled about her head, would forever be etched in his brain.

"I'm glad."

Her finger moved upward until it was smoothing across his lower lip.

"I've only been with one other man in my life, Rafe. And that was a few years ago. I'm sorry if I—well, seemed rusty."

His hands splayed against her back then slid slowly down to her buttocks. "Hmm. I'm almost afraid to think what you might be with a little practice."

She smiled then bending her head, she kissed him, and as Rafe kissed her back it dawned on him that something was different. He was different. Lilly had just given him incredibly hot sex, yet that wasn't enough for him. He wanted to hold her, feel her cheek resting against his chest and listen to her soft breathing. Not for just a moment or two, but for the whole night and endless nights to come.

"Maybe you can help me practice," she replied in a sensual, teasing voice.

She wasn't being serious and that was a good thing, he thought. Neither one of them wanted strings or attachments. Still, it was nice to hear her say something to make this night seem more than just a onetime wonder.

"I think I can handle that. And more," he added.

She pressed a quick kiss to his lips then rested her head upon his shoulder. Rafe closed his eyes and tried not to think too far beyond the moment. Even so, his thoughts were already jumping into the future. And though he knew he would eventually have to let this woman go, his mind refused to picture it.

"I've not eaten supper," she murmured. "Have you?"

"No. Greta had cooked lasagna, but I didn't wait around to eat. I was more intent on seeing you."

He gently stroked his fingertips down her spine and she responded with a sigh so soft it was barely discernible.

Her voice drowsy, she said, "After the day I've had today I never expected it to turn out this nice."

"The emergency room was busy today?"

"Yes. And I'm fine with that. I like helping people. But I had a run-in with one of the E.R. doctors. He says he's going to report me."

"Does that worry you?"

"No. I was in the right. Besides, I'm friendly with the director of nursing. He'll listen to my side of things. I just hate getting angry. My mother is always flying off the handle. So I try my best not to be like her. But today Doctor Sherman pushed my temper button."

The idea of anyone mistreating Lilly made him want to carry her to the ranch and keep her there. But he couldn't do that any more than he could start telling her how to deal with her job or her coworkers. For one thing he didn't have that right. No more than she had the right to try and control his life. Still, the idea of any man trying to bully or hurt Lilly brought out a fierce protectiveness he'd never felt toward any woman before.

"Well, don't feel bad about losing your temper. I had a set-to with my brother Finn today. And to make matters worse, I was the one doing all the ranting. He sat there listening and never raised his voice."

His confession had her scrambling to a sitting position. "You had an argument with Finn? About what?"

"Horses. Half the remuda is out of commission because of injuries or sickness. Finn has been promising to purchase more to add to the string, but he keeps dallying. This morning I got so fed up I chewed him out about it."

Confusion puckered her brow. "But all those horses

you showed me that were stalled in the barn—can't you use some of those out on the range?"

"Those aren't working horses," he explained. "They're in training for cutting and Western pleasure prospects."

"Oh, I see," she said thoughtfully, then bending closer, she trailed gentle fingers alongside his face. "I'm sorry you had cross words with your brother, but I'm sure it will get better."

She wasn't recriminating or judgmental. Instead, she was encouraging him and somehow that made him feel even guiltier about the episode with Finn.

"I'm going to make sure that it does," he said. Pulling her back down beside him, he kissed her swollen lips and tangled his fingers in her silky hair. "Being with you like this makes everything better."

Stretching out beside him, she pillowed her cheek upon his shoulder. "For me, too, Rafe."

He'd never had this sort of pillow talk with a woman before. Normally, he would already have been up and dressed and thinking of a good excuse to say goodnight. Was this the way it was with married couples? he wondered. Not that he'd ever consider becoming Lilly's husband. But he could certainly get used to having this precious time with her.

"That's why we need more time together." He spoke his thoughts aloud. "I wish you'd move out to the ranch."

That jerked her head up and she stared at him. "I couldn't!"

He studied the incredulous look on her face. "Why not? You're already out there every day to give Gramps his therapy. Wouldn't it be nice to simply get up and walk upstairs instead of driving for thirty minutes?"

"I'd still have to drive into town for my shift at the hospital," she argued.

As far as Rafe was concerned he wished she'd forget about working in the emergency room. But she wasn't the type who'd ever give up her independence. And Rafe was smart enough not to mention the idea. Besides, he could see her work was important to her. And that made it important to him.

"If you stayed on the ranch, that would cut out one of the trips," he reasoned. "And you did enjoy staying in the green room, didn't you?"

"It was very nice," she agreed. "But Bart isn't going to need therapy for a whole lot longer. At the most, maybe four or five more weeks. Besides, me staying in the green room would never work. You'd end up in my bed or I'd end up in yours."

"Naturally," he said with a grin.

She shook her head. "I couldn't deal with that. Not in your family's house. It wouldn't be decent or right."

"They'd never have to know."

She frowned at him. "I'd know."

Before he could say any more on the subject, she scooted off the bed and began plucking her clothing off the floor.

Sensing that he might have angered her, he asked, "Where are you going?"

Her expression coy, she tossed his boxers at him. "Just stay where you are. I'll be back in a few minutes."

Considering the fact that his body felt like he'd just run a marathon, it was easy for Rafe to promise, "I'll be right here."

A few minutes later, she returned wearing a red silk

kimono and carrying a small tray stacked with sandwiches, cookies and two cups of coffee.

She flashed him a tempting smile. "You talked about
me taking coffee in bed. Well, it's your turn."

While she placed the tray on the nightstand, he scooted
up and rested his back against the headboard.

Handing him a cup of the coffee, she said, "There's
bologna or ham. Take your pick."

Grinning, he chose a triangle of ham and bread. "I've
never had this kind of supper before. What if I get crumbs
in the bed?"

She chuckled. "I doubt we'll notice."

He patted the empty space next to him. "Aren't you
going to join me?"

"I wouldn't miss it." Climbing over him, she propped
a pillow against the headboard then settled herself next
to him.

He handed her the other cup and a sandwich, then
watched her bite hungrily into the snack.

"Why didn't you tell me you were going to make us
something to eat? I would've helped you."

"I wanted to surprise you. Besides, I figured you probably didn't know your way around the kitchen."

He feigned an insulted look. "Well, I know how to do
this much. Mom showed us boys how to do a few things
to feed ourselves."

She reached across him and plucked another sandwich from the tray. "Hmm. That surprises me. I would've
thought you boys were always outside on a horse or playing with bugs or lizards."

"Boys love to eat, too." He slanted her a sensual
glance. "But you seemed to have figured that out."

"Did you and your brothers get along when you were young, or did you fuss and fight?" she asked.

"Mostly, we all got along. And still do. Except for a few incidents like today when I jumped Finn. But when I lose my temper it's because of my work—the ranch. No other reason."

"That's because it's so important to you."

Amazed, he looked at her. No woman had ever been able to read him before, yet Lilly seemed to instinctively understand what he was all about. The notion jolted him. That was the sort of thing a man looked for in a wife. He wanted his woman to know who he was deep inside and what was most important to him. But Rafe didn't want a wife. He didn't need that complication or worry.

He swallowed a bite of the sandwich before he answered. "When Gramps made me foreman, he threw a heavy load onto my shoulders. I was only twenty-five. It's not easy stepping in and bossing men twice your age who have worked as a ranch hand all their lives."

"Mmm. I'm sure there was some resentment."

"Resentment, hell. Some of them were downright angry with me. I got the job because I was the owner's grandson—that's what they all believed. Never mind the fact that I'd been working alongside them ever since I was big enough to ride a horse or hold a rope in my hand."

Glancing at him over the rim of her cup, she asked frankly, "Did you get the job because Bart is your grandfather?"

He was learning more and more that she didn't mince words. Nor did she try to feed his ego like most of the women he'd known in the past. And there were times like right now that her bluntness took him aback and forced him to view things in a different perspective.

"Geez, Lilly, what kind of question is that?"

"An honest one. I'm sorry if it offended you."

He swallowed the last of his sandwich before he replied, "I'm not offended. Actually, it's partly the truth. I probably never would've gotten a chance at the position at that age if I'd not been a Calhoun. I'll admit, I was privileged in that way. But that didn't make me less qualified for the job."

Her gaze continued to study his face and his heart swelled as he watched admiration fill her brown eyes.

"I've gotten to know Bart pretty well. He wouldn't hire any man unless he was sure the man could do the job. Apparently, your grandfather had plenty of confidence in you."

His gaze dropped to the brown liquid in his cup. "I often wondered what prompted Gramps to make me foreman of the Silver Horn. And sometimes I ask myself if he gave me the job as a test. One that he thought I would fail. Or maybe he was trying to punish me for not being the sort of man he wanted."

Frowning, she leaned across him once again to place her cup on the nightstand, and his senses were immediately snared by her feminine scent and the warmth of her smooth skin.

"And what does Bart expect of you?" she asked as she settled back against the headboard.

He shrugged and then before he could stop it, he could feel a blush spread up his neck and onto his face. "More serious. More settled. He and my dad don't like the fact that I—uh—enjoy women as much as I do. Or did," he added quickly, then realizing how that sounded, he groaned. "That sounded bad, didn't it?"

To his surprise, she laughed softly. "Rafe, it's not like

you're admitting to something I didn't already know. You've had girlfriends. I'm not expecting you to consider me your one and only."

If any other woman had said that to him, he would have been happy, but coming from Lilly, it was like a knife blade between his ribs. He wanted her to think of him as her one and only. He couldn't bear to think of any other man being with her the way he was with her now. What in hell was going on with him? he wondered. Whatever it was, he didn't like the uncomfortable way it was making him feel. But he couldn't seem to stop it.

Placing his cup next to hers on the nightstand, he shifted around on the bed so that he was facing her. "You mean—you wouldn't mind if I—dated some other woman?" he asked guardedly.

Her expression suddenly sober, she glanced away from him and shrugged. "Like we said, Rafe, no strings. Nothing serious."

That was exactly what they'd agreed on, he thought. But damn it, he didn't want any other woman. And he sure as hell didn't want her with another man. But he couldn't start preaching that to her now. He'd already told her that he wasn't the jealous sort. That would make him sound like he was becoming possessive and God help him—in love.

"Yeah. Nothing serious," he said in a low, gruff voice. "Only pleasure."

Her gaze cut back to his face and then as a smile slowly spread across her own face, she reached for him. "That's what I want to give you, Rafe."

Wrapping his arms around her, he lowered his mouth to hers and as the heated contact between their lips warmed his body, he felt it tightening with need.

Moments later, when he finally pulled his mouth away to catch his breath, he murmured, "I really should be getting out of this bed and be going home."

Nibbling on the lobe of his ear, she whispered. "Is anyone waiting for you there?"

Desire was already shooting through him, shoving common sense to a dark, shadowy corner of the bedroom and sending his libido into overload. "No."

Her lips were suddenly hovering over his. "Then why don't you stay with me tonight?"

He'd never stayed with any woman all night. That was the same as saying *I like you very much—I want to be with you for more than a few minutes or even an hour or two—I might want something that lasts longer. Maybe even to be with you like a man is with his wife.*

Groaning with surrender, he tried to blank that last thought from his mind. "You're making it very hard for me to say no."

Her soft laugh fanned his cheeks. "That's my intention."

Closing his eyes, he rolled onto his back and pulled her over on top of him. And as she slid onto him, he was certain he'd never be the same man again. Minute by minute she was taking pieces of him that he would never get back.

## Chapter Eight

Three days later, Lilly was sitting across a desk from Chet Anderson, the director of nursing for Tahoe General. In his late thirties, he was an attractive man with dark brown hair and eyes to match. She'd heard rumors that his wife divorced him several years ago, but she'd never discussed anything that private with the man. And though he routinely asked her for a date, she'd only accepted one time and that had been for an innocent lunch at the hospital cafeteria.

This morning, however, he'd not summoned her to his office to ask her to dinner. Even though he was smiling at her like the thought was on his mind.

"Look, Lilly, I really didn't call you up here to give you a lecture." Picking up a white coffee mug, he leaned back in his desk. "I know what you're dealing with. Doctor Sherman is a pain in the butt. And if it was left up to me, he'd be gone from this hospital before the day ended. Unfortunately, I don't have the authority to hire and fire doctors."

Crossing her legs, she carefully smoothed the hem of her skirt over her knee. "I'm sorry, Chet. I shouldn't have said anything to Doctor Sherman. But sending a patient to surgery on a hunch that something is broken is shabby doctoring, if you ask me."

"He says he was trying to cut costs."

"At that point the patient wasn't concerned about cost. He was more worried about being cut unnecessarily!"

"I have no doubt about that."

"Sherman thinks of himself as a diagnostic genius. And perhaps he is, but we're supposed to follow the proper procedures with our patients here at Tahoe." Pausing, she shook her head with regret. "Even so, I should have handled the situation with a little more tact. Now you've had to listen to Sherman ranting and raving about a disobedient nurse. And I deeply apologize for that."

"You are one of the best RNs this hospital has, Lilly. I trust you to always do the right thing. Don't worry about Sherman," he said dismissively. "I'll deal with him. He won't like it. But I think he and I will come to some understanding. And if he gives you any more trouble just come to me. I'll take care of him."

"Thank you, Chet. I promise I'll try to keep my cool around the man. And if I have anything to say to him, I'll make sure I don't do it in front of a patient." Scooting to the edge of the chair, she started to rise, only to have him immediately wave her back down. "Is there something else?"

"Not about Sherman," he said. "I can't let you out of my office without asking you if you'd like to have dinner one night. Maybe tomorrow night?"

Chet Anderson would be a great catch for any woman and she genuinely liked the man. But he didn't make her heart go pitter-patter. When she looked at him, she couldn't imagine touching him in the ways she'd touched Rafe, feeling the things she'd felt with Rafe.

"I—uh—it's nice of you to ask, Chet. But I'm—well, I'm seeing someone right now."

*Seeing?* Using that word to describe her relationship with Rafe was laughable, she thought. She'd had mind-blowing sex with the man. Yet even now she was still trying to figure out what had made her succumb to Rafe's advances in the first place. Why had she jumped straight into the fire with both feet?

"Oh. Lucky guy. I hope he's being good to you."

Good? Rafe was a bad boy in a very good way, she thought, as a wave of heat touched her face. But she had no idea how long he would be good to her. And for right now she wasn't letting herself think too much about tomorrow. She'd made the mistake of pinning her future on a man once before. She'd never do that again. And yet the future kept looming in front of her, daring her to think about the long-term and if Rafe could possibly be a part of it.

"He is."

Leaning forward, he studied her closely. "Well, until he puts a wedding ring on your finger, I won't give up."

Taken completely off guard by his comment, she said, "I seriously doubt that's going to happen with him—or any man. Now I'd better get back to work. Marcella is handling things by herself. She probably needs me."

With a strange little pain niggling the middle of her chest, she quickly rose to her feet and started to the door.

"Lilly."

With her hand on the knob, she paused and glanced back at him.

He said quietly, "We never know what the future might bring. I just want you to be happy."

*Future. Happy.* Lilly wasn't about to tie those two words together. Her heart could only deal with one day at a time. With a wan smile, she said, "Thanks, Chet. I'll remember that."

At the same time, nearly twenty miles away on the Silver Horn, Rafe was in the tack room, searching through a stack of mohair girths, when a footstep sounded behind him and then Finn called out.

"Rafe, I've been hunting all over the place for you. I saw Denver out at the saddling paddock but he didn't know where you'd gotten off to."

Rafe tossed the girths over an empty saddle rack and looked around at his brother. "My girth is about to break. I'm trying to find a thirty-four inch. That should fit Roscoe."

Finn walked closer and Rafe didn't miss the rueful expression on his face. Since they'd argued the other day, Rafe hadn't had a chance to talk to his younger brother. Now was as good a time as any to apologize, he decided.

"I'm glad you found me," Rafe went on. "I've wanted to speak with you. In private."

Finn began, "If you're worried about the horse situation I—"

"Before you say anything else, Finn, I want to apologize. I shouldn't have been so hard on you. I know you're trying and I know it's not easy to find quality stock. And I'm short on patience."

His eyes wide, Finn stepped forward and placed a

hand on Rafe's forehead. "My God, you must be sick," he teased.

Rafe playfully swatted his brother's hand away. "I'm not sick. I'm trying to be fair. So don't push your luck, little brother."

Grinning now, Finn rocked back on the heels of his boots. "Well, since you're being so nice about it, I've got good news to share with you. I made a deal with the Sandbur for twelve horses. They should arrive here on the Horn by Friday."

"That's only two days away! This is great news, Finn. Did you tell Denver?"

"No. I wanted you to be the first to know."

Feeling more than sheepish, Rafe turned and began to rifle through the girths. "Thanks, Finn. I'm not sure I deserve that from you. But thanks, anyway."

Moving closer, Finn slapped a hand on Rafe's shoulder. "Look, Rafe, I need to apologize to you, too. It's my fault—I should've started rebuilding the remuda sooner. But I was thinking you could manage this spring roundup with the string we had, then purchase more before winter hit, when horse prices normally go down. I wasn't counting on you having that many injured and sick horses."

"Forget it, Finn. I have."

"All right. It's forgotten. But what I said about you and Lilly—that was out of line. Your relationship with her is none of my business."

Dropping the girths, he faced Finn. "You're my brother. You have a right to ask me things."

Frowning, Finn moved a few steps away and took a seat on a bale of hay. "Not in that way. But I am curious about—no, I'm more than curious. I'm concerned about you and her."

Rafe was surprised that Finn had even noticed anything was going on between him and Lilly. Yes, she'd had dinner and stayed that one night on the Horn, but other than that, he'd not told his family exactly how much he'd been seeing Lilly. "Why are you concerned? She's just a girlfriend."

Finn skewered him with a pointed glance. "Really? I've never seen any one of your girlfriends around here before."

"Finn, she's Gramps's nurse. She's here on the ranch most every day, anyway. Besides, why should you be worried about me and Lilly? The woman makes me happy."

"Is that what you call it? Happy?"

The questions rattled through Rafe's thoughts as he stared at his younger brother. "What is *that* supposed to mean?"

Finn shrugged. "I don't know. I can't put my finger on it. But you've not been yourself here lately. And—"

"Just because I got angry about the horses—"

"It isn't that," he interrupted before Rafe could say more. "You've seemed preoccupied—almost troubled. You don't seem happy to me."

Lifting his hat from his head, Rafe slanted fingers through his hair as memories of making love to Lilly began to flash rapid fire through his mind. He supposed Finn was right. He could hardly concentrate on anything but Lilly. Seeing her again, making love to her again, had become his sole focus. She was taking over his life and even if it was in a good way right now, that didn't bode well for the long run of things. Not if he wanted to keep his freedom.

"She's wonderful, Finn. I've never known any woman like her. In fact, she's probably too good for me."

"So you're getting serious about her. Hell, Rafe, out of all my brothers, you're the only one who's sworn off the idea of marriage. How is this thing with Lilly going to work?"

For the past three days that same question had been nagging at Rafe. She'd dismissed the idea of staying here on the ranch and even if she were to ask him, he couldn't move in with her. A majority of the time his job took up sixteen to eighteen hours of the day; he couldn't spend another hour and a half on the road, driving back and forth from her house to the ranch. They'd made a pact to keep things casual, yet the more he was with her, the more his thoughts kept leaping to the future. Something told him that months, even years, would not be long enough to satisfy his cravings for Lilly. And for a man who didn't want the ties of marriage, that was a mighty scary thought.

Drawing a deep breath, Rafe turned back to the girths and grabbed the first one to come loose from the tangled pile. The size no longer mattered; he'd keep adjusting until he made it fit. "I'm not getting serious, Finn. I can't. Lilly doesn't want that and neither do I. There's nothing to make work. We're just enjoying each other's company. That's all."

"Well, if you say so." Finn rose from the hay bale. "But you know something, Rafe, there wouldn't be anything wrong if you did get serious about Lilly. You might figure out that you're husband material after all."

Rafe's chuckle was more cynical than anything. "If I ever get to thinking I'm husband material I'll just take another hard look at Dad. That'll jerk me back to reality."

Clearly confused, Finn asked, "What is that supposed to mean?"

"If you don't understand then you're better off not

knowing." With girth in hand, he stepped past his brother and headed out the door. "Gotta go. Denver is waiting on me."

The next morning Lilly was climbing the stairs to Bart's study when she heard the jingle of spurs, and then a pair of hands suddenly grabbed her from behind.

Squealing with fright, she twisted around to see Rafe's laughing face, and she playfully pummeled her fists against his broad chest.

"That was a mean trick! You scared the heck out of me!"

"Sorry. I didn't mean to frighten you. I was trying to catch you before you went into Gramps." The amusement on his face dissolved as he wrapped his arms around her shoulders and quickly brought his mouth down to hers. Lilly could do nothing but kiss him back and wonder how she'd gone for nearly four days without making love to the man.

When he finally lifted his head, he murmured, "I've been desperate to see you."

"We had lunch together at the Green Lizard three days ago during my work break. And I've been here every morning," she pointed out.

He frowned. "Having lunch with you was very nice. But it's not the same as being alone with you. And for the past two mornings, I've had to head out early. We've been moving a herd of bulls over on the Red Canyon range."

His hands were moving against her back, filling her body with delicious warmth and making it extremely hard to concentrate on his words. "Finished now?" she asked.

"No. We plan on wrapping up that job today. But I'll

be free tomorrow afternoon. I wanted to see if you could get off work for a few hours."

Her smile coy, her fingers played with the tails of the red bandanna tied around his neck. Since they'd made love that night at her house, her body had been aching, craving to be close to him. Now that she was finally touching him again, she didn't want to let him go. "I just happen to be off tomorrow afternoon and tomorrow night."

"You're not kidding me, are you?"

"No. Why? You have a plan to take me to the Sierra Chateau again?"

He frowned with disbelief. "No. Do you want to go there again?"

"I was teasing, Rafe. I'd rather be—" she glanced around to make sure no one else was nearby, then finished "—somewhere alone with you."

"Funny how you seem to know exactly what I want to hear." He kissed her then pulled back just enough to mouth against her lips. "I'm going to take you riding. To a quiet, beautiful place where it will be just the two of us. And maybe a few flowers and birds and butterflies."

"Mmm. Sounds heavenly."

"Great. I'll see you tomorrow, then. I should be finished by noon, so come as soon as you can."

As he eased her out of his arms, she asked, "You have to leave now? I thought you might visit with me while I work with Bart. He'd love your company and so would I," she said.

"And I'd love to stay, but the men are waiting on me." He lifted the back of her hand to his lips. "I'll make it up to you tomorrow. Promise."

Her heart dancing with joy, she smiled at him. "I'll make sure you keep that promise."

He gave her one last kiss, then hurried down the stairs. Lilly watched him until he was out of sight then climbed the last two steps to the landing.

"So that's why you're late. You've been dallying around with my grandson."

Jerking her head in the direction of Bart's room, she saw the older man was standing in the open doorway, leaning heavily on his cane.

She marched toward him. "Bart! What are you doing? Spying on your nurse?"

"Spying, hell! Greta told me you'd left the kitchen ten minutes ago. I was trying to see if you'd fallen off the landing or something."

Considering that his daughter-in-law had died from a fall on that very staircase, Lilly could hardly scold the man for being overly dramatic.

"I'm sorry if I worried you, Bart. Rafe caught me on the staircase and—"

"Yes, I could see how he caught you," he said with a roll of his eyes, then slowly and carefully he turned and maneuvered his way back into the room.

Lilly supposed she should have been embarrassed to have Bart catch her kissing his grandson, but she wasn't. She and Rafe were both unattached adults.

"What are you doing with my grandson, Lilly? Making a fool out of him?"

Lilly pressed her lips together as she waited for Bart to sit down in his easy chair. "I couldn't do that even if I tried," she told the older man.

"Hmm. I wouldn't be so sure. Look at what you've got me doing."

Lilly gave him a clever smile. "That's only because you want to get back to being your old self. And you're smart enough to know that if you do as I say you'll get there."

She sank onto a footstool near Bart's chair and he motioned toward a breakfast tray sitting on an end table to his left.

"Let's have a little coffee before we start."

"All right. But don't get the idea that you're stalling. Your exercise clock won't start until you do."

Grinning slyly, he filled a china cup and added a dollop of cream before handing it to her. "You're just like my late wife, Gilda. Always a stickler for staying on schedule."

She took an appreciative sip while leisurely regarding him over the rim of her cup. Bart was continuing to make remarkable progress and the more she worked with him, the more she could see where the Calhoun family found its strength and determination. Everyone, including Chet Anderson, who'd personally asked her to take on this job, had warned her that she was in for a difficult time and described Bart as a mean SOB. But thankfully, she'd yet to see that side of the man. In fact, from the very first day she'd met Bart, she'd felt a connection to him. Just as she'd felt a connection to Rafe, only in a different way.

"You like my grandson that much, do you?" he asked bluntly.

Lilly nodded. "He's a pretty special guy."

Bart shook his head. "You surprise me, Lilly. I just didn't think you were the type to fall for Rafe's blarney. I thought you were wiser than that."

How bad could it be, she wondered, to have his own grandfather deem him an unsuitable boyfriend for her?

"You were wise enough to make him the foreman of the Silver Horn. That tells me how you really regard your grandson."

He stroked his chin with his thumb and forefinger. "Rafe is a damned good cowboy. No one has to tell him what needs to be done on the ranch. Even when he was only a boy, he understood what it took to keep things running smoothly. When he took on the foreman job, it took him a while to learn how to handle the men without making them hate him. That's come along, too." His gaze settled on Lilly's face. "But being a good cowboy and responsible foreman doesn't mean he's worthy company for a woman. When it comes to females he's never had a serious bone in his body."

"I understand that, Bart. And I'm okay with it. Because I'm not looking for a husband."

Even though he didn't make an immediate reply, Lilly could see she'd surprised him. And why not? Rafe was a very eligible bachelor. Plenty of women would give their eye teeth to marry a man who was handsome, sexy and unbelievably wealthy. And maybe now that Bart had seen her kissing Rafe, he was worried she had the idea of marrying into the Calhoun fortune.

"That isn't normal, Lilly. You ought to want a husband and children."

Grimacing, she took another sip of coffee. "Why? Why do I need a husband and children? I'm just fine like I am."

He snorted. "You're all woman, Lilly. With a woman's wishes. Go fool someone else, 'cause I'm not buying."

She took one last drink from her cup then returned it to the tray. "Bart, you needn't worry that I'm after

Rafe's share of the Calhoun fortune. Money has never interested me."

His jaw clamped tight. "You're making me mad as hell, young lady. The idea of you being after money never crossed my mind. I'm concerned about you. Not any damned Calhoun money!"

Shaking her head at him, she said, "All right, Bart. There's no need for you get riled up or concerned. I'm here to make you healthy again. Not give you a setback."

"Then you need to mind what I'm trying to tell you. Rafe is a rascal. He'll break your heart. I don't want to see that happen, Lilly. I've grown quite fond of you and it would hurt me to know that my grandson ever made you unhappy."

As a small girl, both sets of Lilly's grandparents had lived far away and her visits to them had been limited. And by the time she'd gone to work as a nurse, both grandfathers had passed away from health problems. Being around Bart made her think about both men and how much she missed not having them in her life. She also wondered if they'd be as ready to give her as much advice as Bart.

Her throat tight with emotion, she leaned forward and placed her hand on his arm. "I'm fond of you, too, Bart. And I promise, you don't need to worry about me. I can deal with Rafe's rascally ways."

The next afternoon when Lilly met Rafe at the horse barn, Bart's words of warning were far from her mind. The sky was azure-blue, the wind a gentle caress and Rafe's smiles were full of adventure as he helped her into the saddle.

"I thought your horse was gray," she said as they reined their mounts away from the barn.

"Oh, you're talking about Roscoe. He's been working hard and needs a rest today. This dun is Finn's horse, Gunsmoke. Normally, my brother doesn't allow anyone to touch him, but he felt like he owed me a favor."

As their horses walked slowly abreast, Lilly looked at him with interest. "I take that to mean you resolved your differences?"

"We did. Twelve new horses for the working remuda are arriving tomorrow. I can hardly wait to see them."

The excitement in his voice had her smiling. "Well, I hope today you're not so preoccupied with thoughts of the new horses that you forget about me," she teased.

"Not a chance." Grinning, his gaze swept up and down her body. "You're looking too cute to forget for even one minute. Where did you get that hat? It looks like someone sat on it."

Reaching up, she adjusted the crumpled straw cowboy hat to a lower angle on her forehead. "I've had it for years. Since I was a teenager and rode horses with—"

"Don't tell me. Blue Bravo."

She playfully wrinkled her nose at him. "I should've never told you about Blue. Especially since I've never heard you talk about any of your girlfriends."

"That's because I never had one for more than a day or two. I didn't have a longtime companion like you."

Blue had been a companion, she thought, while Grant had been something else. More like an obsession, she supposed. So what was Rafe becoming to her? She didn't want to try to answer that now. It was too complicated and this day was too special to ruin it with a serious contemplation.

"Hmm. I think I should warn you that your grandfather saw us kissing on the staircase yesterday. He keeps warning me that you're a rascal. I assured him that I know what you are."

He frowned. "Gee, thanks for making me sound like a real stand-up guy."

She laughed then glanced around to notice they were nearing the end of the working ranch yard. Ahead of them was a far stretch of open range surrounded on two sides by a ridge of mountains.

"So where are we going?"

"West. That's all I'm going to tell you for right now," he said slyly.

"Just remember I've not ridden for over a year," she warned him. "I'm not up to a marathon."

"Don't worry, sweet Lilly. We're not going on a marathon. Just a little adventure."

She'd been on an adventure from the very first day she'd met this man, Lilly thought. He was changing her life and she had to believe he was changing it for the better.

For the next forty minutes they rode at a leisurely pace until they reached a stand of foothills that Rafe called Eagle's Ridge. On a narrow cattle trail, they began to climb upward through a sparse stand of lodgepole pine separated by steep slopes covered with short green grass. Farther along, huge boulders jutted from the ground and the dirt trail grew rockier. To Lilly's relief, her mount, a little sorrel mare with a blaze face, was very sure-footed and picked her way carefully over the loose surface.

Eventually, the trail reached the crest of the mountain and Rafe reined his horse to a stop in the shade of an enormous white fir tree. Lilly pulled up alongside him and pushed a hand against the small of her back.

"That was quite a climb," she said. "How much farther are we going?"

He looked at her with concern. "Not far. Are you too tired to go on?"

She shook her head. "No. But I will be ready for a rest. Are we still on Silver Horn land?"

His smile was indulgent. "Lilly, if you rode all day in any direction from the house, you'd never get off Horn land."

"I should have known that," she said with a shake of her head, then glanced around her at the tall fir trees, the slabs of rocks and sprouts of pink and yellow wildflowers bending in the breeze. "It's no wonder you love this place so much. It's beautiful."

She looked over to see he was gazing at her and his expression was soft and gentle, so much so that gazing back at him tightened her throat with emotion. Dear Lord, he wasn't supposed to be affecting her this way, she thought. She wasn't supposed to be feeling this much for him or letting herself imagine the two of them riding together long after they'd turned old and gray.

"It makes me happy that you appreciate the land, Lilly. Happier than you could ever know."

"And it makes me happy that you're showing it to me. So we're even," she said huskily.

Reaching over, he briefly touched her cheek then clucked to his horse. "Follow me. We're almost to our destination," he told her.

With the trail turning to steep switchbacks, the descent to the bottom of the ridge took twenty minutes. By the time they reached flat ground, Lilly was definitely ready to dismount. Her legs were trembling with fatigue and her back was aching, but the pain was instantly forgotten as the horses stepped into an open meadow full of tall grass and patches of red and purple wildflowers.

"This is spectacular, Rafe! This must be our stopping spot."

"Not yet." He pointed toward a line of trees on the opposite side of the meadow. "We're going there."

"But Rafe, this meadow is gorgeous and the horses can graze here. Let's get down."

He shook his head, which prompted her to groan.

"All right," she conceded. "But I'm warning you. This next place better be good!"

He chuckled. "Don't worry. We'll take some time to visit the meadow, too."

Mollified by his promise, she nudged the sorrel forward and followed him to the stand of trees. Once they entered the shady canopy, she could hear the sound of trickling water.

Down a short trail to the left, the trees suddenly opened up to a wide creek where knee-deep water tumbled over large boulders and bleached, fallen logs. In places, willows grew along the creek bank, while other spots were filled with cattails and Indian paintbrush.

A few feet away from the water's edge, Rafe dismounted Gunsmoke then helped her down from the saddle.

Once she was standing on the ground his hands lingered on the sides of her waist and Lilly was grateful for the support.

"I thought I was in pretty good shape," she said with a little laugh. "But my legs feel like two flimsy twigs."

"Riding uses muscles you don't know you have. You need to be doing this more. Think you can walk okay?"

"Sure. I'm not that bad off."

He loosened the girths on both horses and dropped their reins so both animals could move freely to get a drink or nip at the grass.

"They'll stick close by," he assured her. He lifted a pair of saddlebags from his mount then motioned for her to follow him.

After skirting around a pair of tall fir trees, they came face-to-face with a huge boulder blocking the path.

"What now? Am I supposed to turn into a squirrel and scamper over that thing?"

He laughed. "Either climb rock or wade water. Take your pick."

"You didn't bring me on a leisurely ride. You brought me on a death march," she joked.

Laughing, he said, "C'mon. I'll help you over."

A minute later, they were standing safely on the other side and Lilly was staring around her in complete wonder. A string of head-high boulders created a U shape that opened to the creek. The flat surface inside the hidden space was several yards wide and covered with a carpet of thick green grass. Wildflowers grew along the base of the rocks and higher along the tiny fissures of cracks created by years of eroding wind and water. Above their heads boughs of white fir and pine created fingers of cool shade and filled the air with the pungent scent of evergreen.

"Oh, my," she said in a low, awe-filled voice. "I thought the meadow was gorgeous, but this is incredible. Rafe. It's like a hidden room with a view of the creek."

"I have many favorite spots on the ranch. But this

one is at the top of my list." He glanced at her. "Do you really like it?"

"I love it! It's like we're almost in another world."

He dropped the saddlebags to the ground and reached for her. Lilly went all too willingly in his arms and as the front of her body settled against his, she sighed with undisguised pleasure.

"I've been dreaming about having you here with me, Lilly. With no phones or people. No sounds except the birds and the wind in the pines."

He pushed the hat from her head and the stampede string caught against her throat and caused the crumpled straw to dangle against her back. With the headgear out of the way, he thrust his fingers into her hair and combed the flattened strands back from her face.

Lilly's heart quickened and suddenly it didn't matter that her legs were spongy and her mouth dry from thirst. Making love to Rafe was all that her mind could focus on and she tilted her face invitingly up to his.

"Make love to me, Rafe."

Her whispered plea barely had time to pass her lips before his head dropped and he captured her mouth in an all-consuming kiss.

The contact was like throwing a lighted match into a pool of gasoline. The combustion was instant and fire flashed between them, welding their bodies tightly together. And just as she began to think her legs were going to collapse, he lowered them both to the ground.

The grass was soft and cool and the scent of it combined with Rafe's to fill her head. As he began to remove her clothes, she was vaguely aware of the dappled sunlight above them, the soft breeze and the faint sound of rushing water. But by the time the last garment was tossed aside, her senses were whirling too fast to comprehend her surroundings. All she knew was that his lips were plundering hers, his hands touching her everywhere, sending ripples of fire through every cell in her body.

When his fingers slipped between her thighs and found the aching, moist spot inside her, she groaned with a mixture of agony and pleasure. He probed the heated depths until she was writhing against him and just when she thought she was going to splinter into a thousand pieces, he unzipped his jeans and entered her with a frantic thrust.

The two of them hardly had enough time to settle into a rhythm before they both exploded into mindless ecstasy that had them clutching each other close and straining to merge their bodies into one.

And when awareness did finally make a flickering return to Lilly's mind, the thought struck her that she was lost to this man. Totally and irrevocably lost.

## Chapter Nine

Minutes later, after Lilly had time to collect her senses, she pulled on her shirt and panties then stretched out next to Rafe on the grass. With her cheek pillowed against her arm, she gazed at Rafe, who was resting on his back with his arms folded behind his head. His eyes were half-closed and the rise and fall of his chest was barely discernible. He was more relaxed than she'd ever seen him and as she studied his sexy image, her thoughts went beyond what she could see.

Had their heated connection rocked him as much as it had her? Even though she would've liked to know the answer, she wasn't about to present the question to him. The only thing she was supposed to be interested in was the physical pleasure he could give her. But oh, the tender thoughts of longing going through her mind were traveling straight to her heart. And she didn't have a clue as to how to make them take a detour.

After a while, she couldn't help but voice a thread of her thoughts. "Rafe, why do you think there aren't any women in your family home?"

The question drew his face toward her and he studied her through lazy eyes. "I never thought about it. Why do you ask?"

She sighed. "Oh, I was thinking about Bart finding us kissing yesterday. I believe it was a little shocking to him. None of your brothers have wives. And neither your father nor grandfather show any interest in finding another wife. There isn't any kind of romantic affection going on in your home."

"You already know that my father and grandfather lost their wives. And as for us brothers—we aren't necessarily looking for lasting romance."

She didn't know his brothers well enough to form an opinion about their views on love and marriage. But she didn't have to wonder about Rafe's stance on the subject. He'd made it clear from the very start that he wasn't a marrying man. Still, his words hurt. He'd made love to her as though she were everything to him. And always would be. But clearly, once the heat of his passion was doused, he reverted back to his bachelor mentality.

*There's nothing wrong with that, Lilly. You don't want to get married, either. You've watched your parents battle it out for years. And you don't want a man to pretend to want marriage, the way that Grant had pretended. Brutal or not, Rafe's honesty is better than that.*

"Why is that? And I'm not talking about you now—but the others. Have any of your brothers ever been married?"

"No. Clancy got close once. To a girl he met in college. But that fell apart and I guess the whole thing soured him on love. I think Evan has always been too caught up in being a lawman to focus on any one woman. Out of all of us, Finn is the most likely family man, but right now his whole life is horses, and little Bowie has been married to the marines for the past seven years."

Lilly silently considered everything he'd said and all the things he'd not said. Particularly about himself.

She said, "The ranch house is a very quiet place. I noticed that the very first day I came to work with Bart. You're probably not going to like me saying this, Rafe, but to me most of the rooms have a bit of a sad feeling."

His gaze dropped from hers as he reached over and trailed a finger down the edge of her unbuttoned shirt. "It wasn't always that way, Lilly. Back when Mom was alive, there were always things going on. Music playing. Friends visiting. And parties were a routine thing. Most of all there was laughter—from all of us."

As Lilly studied his solemn face, her heart contracted. More than anything she wanted Rafe to be truly happy. The sort of happiness that came from deep within. Did that mean she was falling in love with him? That he meant more to her than even her own well-being? The questions disturbed her so much that she closed her eyes and tried to shut them from her mind.

"Your mother wouldn't have wanted that. In fact, I think she'd be downright angry if she knew that her family had let her wonderful home change into a somber tomb."

"You're probably right, Lilly. But losing Mom took the joy out of our home. I don't know how to get it back any more than my brothers do. And Dad—well, he just goes through the motions of living."

Opening her eyes, she gave him a gentle smile. "Well,

I hope that someday all of you figure out how to get the joy back in your home. I want that for you—very much."

The light in his gray eyes was soft and tender as he rolled toward her and pulled her into his arms.

"Lilly, darling. You make me happy. More than I ever thought possible." He pressed a kiss against her forehead, then trailed his parted lips over her cheeks and nose before finally settling them against her lips. "I have snacks and a thermos of coffee in my saddlebags. What do you say we eat and then go explore the meadow?"

"Right now?"

She could feel his lips move into a grin. "Well, I think we could tend to other things first. If you'd like."

"I'd like," she whispered, then groaned with pleasure as his mouth crushed down on hers.

Two weeks later, the month of May was nearing its end and since their ride to the rock cove, the weather had turned unseasonably hot. And though it seemed impossible, their relationship had grown even hotter than the weather. Somehow, sandwiched between their busy jobs, she and Rafe had managed to see each other on a steady basis. They'd even taken in a movie one evening and a few nights after that Rafe had treated her to a special dinner at the Sierra Chateau and followed it up with hours of dancing.

The enjoyable time they'd spent together away from her house and out of her bed had given Lilly hope that Rafe might be beginning to want more from her than just sex. But so far, he'd not put anything like that into words and she could only assume he was satisfied to keep any emotional ties out of their relationship.

When she'd first invited Rafe into her bed, she'd expected the explosive chemistry between them to quickly burn itself out. Instead, she was becoming more and more besotted with the man, and the realization was beginning to fill her with uneasiness. Where did she expect things between them to go? It couldn't go far, she thought dismally. No relationship could last long unless it had a foundation of love holding it together.

After Grant's emotional abuse and the subsequent loss of her baby, she'd convinced herself that she didn't need a permanent man in her life, a soul mate to grow old with. And yet, the idea of Rafe moving on and away from her, which he eventually would, left her feeling more than disenchanted. She couldn't bear to think of him touching a woman the same way he touched her. And the idea that eventually, in the years to come, he might fall in love and marry someone else was like a knife to her heart. So much for not getting serious, she thought miserably.

Trying not to dwell on the subject, she carefully locked the medication cabinet behind her, and after leaving the keys with her supervisor, walked down to a small locker room where the emergency-room nurses stored their personal belongings. In the middle of a shift change, the room was full and for a moment she missed seeing Marcella, who'd worked this evening's shift with her. Then she spotted her in one corner of the room. Her back was turned to the group of nurses and from the dejected droop of her head, Lilly sensed that something was definitely wrong.

Momentarily forgetting about opening her locker, Lilly walked over to the other woman and placed a hand on the back of her shoulder. "Marcella? Why aren't you changing clothes? I thought we were going to go grab a drink together?"

"I'm not sure I'm up to it, Lilly."

The woman's husky voice was about to crack into tears and Lilly swiftly walked around to the front of her.

"What's the matter? Is it that ex of yours pestering you about Harry?"

The auburn-haired woman quickly shook her head. "No. It's nothing to do with him. I've not heard from him in months and I doubt I will."

"Then what's wrong? We were together less than fifteen minutes ago and you were fine then. Did something happen out on the floor? That damned Doctor Sherman wasn't showing his—"

"No. No!" She sniffed then gestured toward the row of lockers lining two walls of the small room. "Let's get changed and get out of here. I'll tell you about it at the Green Lizard."

Fifteen minutes later, the two women were sitting at a small round table, sipping on margaritas and munching on nachos. Marcella had collected herself and was now trying to explain her teary breakdown.

"It's about little Peter," she said. "The boy—"

"I remember," Lilly cut in. "The boy with asthma. What about him? He's not come back to emergency again, has he? I've not seen him on any of my shifts."

"Not on our shifts. But he was admitted yesterday morning to a regular room up on the pediatric ward. I only found out about it a few minutes ago, so I stopped by Doctor Malloy's office to talk to him about the situation."

"Good. Maybe he'll get something done about Peter's welfare."

Groaning, Marcella passed a hand over her forehead. "Seems as though when Peter was brought to E.R. the last time, Doctor Malloy contacted social services. That brought on an investigation and the boy was taken away from his parents due to neglect. From what Doc said, the old grandfather is the only other family Peter has and he's not capable of caring for the child full-time. So that means once the boy gets well enough to leave the hospital, he'll be put in foster care."

"Oh. So aren't you glad about that? At least now he'll be taken care of by—"

"I want to adopt him, Lilly," Marcella interrupted with a rush. "I realize that might be difficult with me being single and all. But I'm a good mother to Harry and I can give Peter a decent home with us."

Completely surprised by Marcella's announcement, Lilly studied her friend's face. "There's no doubt about that, Marcella. But adoption—that's a huge step. To be responsible for a child's life is a serious matter. There's the cost to consider, and Harry's feelings about having a brother. Not to mention the emotional investment you'd be making."

"I understand all that, Lilly. I've been raising Harry on my own for a long time now. I know what being a parent entails. And Harry is already seven. I want more children."

"But you're single," Lilly reasoned.

Marcella grimaced. "So are you. But if you were being totally honest with yourself, Lilly, you'd admit that you'd like to have a child. Even if you don't have a man around to help raise it."

"I don't let myself think about having a baby or a child." And for the most part that was true, Lilly thought. For years after her affair with Grant, she'd done her best to put the idea of having a baby from her mind. But now that Rafe was in her life, every aspect of her thinking seemed to be going awry. The more they made love, the more she could feel a maternal instinct growing inside her. To have his child would be an incredible gift, and the longing to become pregnant hit her at unexpected moments. Even so, she'd never go through another pregnancy alone. And that was exactly what she'd have to do if she ever got pregnant with Rafe's baby. Even if he offered to marry her for the sake of the child, she'd turn him down so quickly his head would spin.

After taking a long sip of her drink, she replied, "I'd be a little abnormal if I didn't think about having a child. But I couldn't do it on my own. Not like you, Marcella. I'm not that strong."

"Bah. You're one of the strongest, most independent women I've ever known."

"Boy, do I ever have you fooled," Lilly muttered drily then reached across the table and squeezed Marcella's hand. "This isn't about me, dear friend. If you're really serious about making Peter a part of your family, then I say go for it."

Tears glistened in her friend's eyes. "Do you really mean that?"

"Every word."

"Thank you, Lilly." She tightened her hold on Lilly's hand. "I don't know how to go about seeking adoption, but I'm going to find out. Since Peter will be put in foster care first, I'll start there."

A thought suddenly struck Lilly. "Marcella, what you need is a lawyer. And I think I know who. Rafe's brother-in-law has a practice here in Carson City. He's also the Calhoun family lawyer. I've heard Rafe speak very highly of the man. I'll bet he'd be glad to help you."

"You think so?"

Lilly gave her a promising smile. "Just leave it to me."

Marcella was about to make a reply when the muffled ring of Lilly's cell phone sounded from inside her clutch purse.

Quickly, she pulled out the device and gave it a swipe to end the noise. Across the table, Marcella said, "If you need to answer that, don't let me bother you."

Lilly shook her head. "It's Rafe. I'll call him when we finish here."

Skeptical now, Marcella asked, "Are you dating him?"

Lilly hadn't mentioned Rafe to her friend in several weeks. Not since that day in the snack room at the hospital and even then she'd not hinted that she had intentions of dating the man. Oh, Lord, so much had happened since then. Her thoughts and plans had changed from not wanting a man in her life, to longing for one every waking moment of the day and to dreaming of a future with him.

She let out a long breath. "Yes. After that day in the snack room and you told me that I shouldn't be punishing him for Grant's mistakes—well, I decided to give the man a chance."

Marcella regarded her thoughtfully. "That was several weeks ago! So how are things developing?"

Staring at the nachos in front of her, Lilly shrugged one shoulder and hoped that Marcella couldn't read the longing on her face. She didn't want her friend to know just how quickly she'd made the reckless decision to mix her life with Rafe's. Or for her to guess just how deeply involved she'd become with him. "We enjoy each other's company and that's as far as it will ever go."

"By your choice or his?"

"Both." Her gaze returning to Marcella, Lilly added, "Rafe isn't interested in marriage."

"And what about you?"

Lilly grimaced. "After Grant? I'm not ready for that kind of risk again. It's better knowing where things stand right off. No hopes. No dreams. No plans. Just one day at a time. I can deal with that. I can't believe in dreamy promises for the future. Not anymore."

"I see. Rafe Calhoun isn't marriage material. He's just a diversion. A pleasure for the moment."

"Absolutely," Lilly told her then reached for her glass to drain the last of her drink, while hoping the alcohol would wash away the fib that had just rolled off her tongue.

Across the table, Marcella pulled the strap of her purse onto her shoulder. "One of these days your past is going to collide with your future, Lilly, and then you're going to realize what's really important to you."

Flipping her long, auburn hair over her shoulder, Marcella rose to her feet. "If you're finished, I need to be getting on. Harry will be watching for me and so will Mom. And you need to call your man."

*Her man.* She supposed she had a right to call him her man. But she'd never be given the chance to call him her husband. And though she'd pretended otherwise to Marcella, that reality was bothering her much more than it should be.

Snatching up her purse, Lilly said, "Let's go. I'll pay us out."

In less than ten minutes she was home, and after kicking off her shoes, she curled up on the end of the couch and punched Rafe's number.

He answered after the first ring. "Lilly, when you didn't answer a few minutes ago, I thought you were probably still at work. Are you?"

"No. When you rang I was with Marcella—having a drink at the Green Lizard."

"You girls must have had a bad shift."

"No. Things were surprisingly light this afternoon and evening. Marcella had some personal things she wanted to talk to me about, that's all. In fact, she needs a lawyer, Rafe, and I mentioned that Jett Sundell was your brother-in-law. Do you think he might help her?"

"Help her with what?"

"She wants to adopt a child who's going to be placed in foster care. I don't know if your brother-in-law deals with that sort of thing, but she would surely appreciate his help."

"Jett deals with all sorts of family law. If you'd like, I'll speak to him about your friend."

"Thanks, Rafe. It would mean a lot to me. Marcella is my best friend—practically my only friend."

"And what am I?" he asked in a low, husky voice. "Aren't I a friend?"

The pit of her stomach fluttered wildly. Just hearing his low, raspy voice and imagining the sensation of his body pressed to hers was enough to muddle her thinking.

"A friend. And more."

"That's what I wanted to hear," he murmured. "Why don't you drive out here to the ranch tonight?"

She wanted to say yes so badly that she very nearly bit her tongue to keep the word inside. "I could. But not to have sex in your father's house. You know how I feel about that."

He growled with disappointment. "We wouldn't have to announce it."

Frustrated, she raked her fingers through her hair.

"So you think sneaking around would make it more acceptable to me?"

"No. I can hear in your voice that it wouldn't." He released a heavy breath. "I have to be up about four in the morning. We discovered a few calves over on the north slope near Eagle's Ridge that we missed during roundup. We'll have to leave early to wind up the job tomorrow. Otherwise, I'd drive into town to see you."

Was it just heated sex that he wanted or did he actually need her company? These past few days, she'd caught herself wondering more and more what she really meant to Rafe and why it should even matter to her.

"Well, if you get your work wrapped up, why don't you come here tomorrow night? My shift ends early so I'll cook supper for you," she offered.

"Hmm. I'll be there. If you can cook as good as you do—other things—then I know it will be delicious."

His provocative suggestion brought a sting of heat to her cheeks and a flash of erotic images dancing through her mind. Yet the images were quickly replaced by Marcella's tearful eyes.

*If you were being totally honest with yourself, Lilly, you'd admit that you'd like to have a child.*

Her friend had touched a spot in her heart that Lilly never wanted to examine or acknowledge. But sooner or later, she was going to be forced to and she could feel that time creeping closer and closer.

Swallowing back a wistful sigh, she said, "Goodbye, Rafe. I'll see you tomorrow night."

"You're hanging up already?" he asked with surprise.

"I'm tired. I'm going to turn in early tonight."

There was a long, awkward pause. "Is anything wrong?"

"Nothing is wrong," she said. Other than the unexplainable urge to cry kept her fighting back a wall of tears. Oh, dear heaven, what was wrong with her? For the first time in years she was behaving like a real woman. She had a man in her life. A man that was filling her days and nights with passion. It would only create problems to try and reach for more. But she wanted more. Far more than Rafe was willing to give.

"All right. I'll see you tomorrow night, then," he said and ended the connection.

After putting her phone aside, Lilly wearily leaned her head back against the couch and let her gaze drift over the living room. Even though the space was small and comfortable, it held no comparison to any of the rooms in the Silver Horn ranch house. If she followed Rafe's wishes, she could be living there in luxury. At least until his desire for her waned and he moved on to the next woman. But luxury didn't interest her. And neither did being Rafe's mistress. She might owe him for waking her from a long, lonely sleep. But now she realized she wanted and deserved more from him.

Something was wrong with Lilly. Although Rafe couldn't put his finger on it, he could feel it in his bones. Maybe she was already growing tired of him. Or maybe she was unhappy because so much of his time was taken up with the ranch. But how could she ask more of him? Her own job required her to work plenty of overtime and with those long hours, it was emotionally taxing. She, more than anyone, ought to understand how important his job was to him.

*You're borrowing trouble, Rafe. Lilly is cooking din-*

*ner for you tonight. The woman wouldn't be going to that*
*much trouble if she was dissatisfied with you.*

Rafe was trying to hang on to that positive thought
when a slight knock sounded on his bedroom door, and
Clancy walked into the room.

"Am I interrupting?" his older brother asked.

Continuing to stuff his shirttail into his jeans, Rafe
shook his head. "No. I'm getting ready to go to town.
What's up?"

"Town? You mean you're going like that?"

He glanced down at his faded jeans, gray chambray
shirt, and scuffed cowboy boots. "What's wrong with
jeans? Lilly would think I was crazy if I showed up in
something dressy."

Rafe looked up to see Clancy staring at him with comical amazement. "To the cattlemen's ball? It's a black-tie
affair, Rafe. Don't you remember?"

"Remember it's black tie? Hell, I didn't even know
about the ball. But it doesn't matter. I'm going to Lilly's
tonight."

His brother hardly looked pleased. "Rafe, this is an
important evening for the local ranchers around here.
Dad is expecting all of us to attend. Evan is even going."

"Good. Then the Calhoun family will be well repre-
sented without me being there."

Rolling his eyes, Clancy walked over to the dresser
and used the mirror to straighten the knot in his tie.
"Rafe, you are the foreman of the Horn! You, out of all
of us Calhouns, should be there tonight."

"Then someone should've had the decency to warn
me about this affair before tonight."

"You're hardly ever around. Dad said he sent you a
text yesterday to remind you."

Rafe wiped a hand over his freshly shaven face. "How the hell am I supposed to receive a text when I'm fifteen miles deep into the mountains—rounding up Horn cattle? You know, someone has to do some actual work around here once in a while. For the past two months I've spent fifteen hours in the saddle for three-fourths of that time. I hardly see spending an evening for myself as a sin!"

Turning away from the mirror, Clancy stood with his hands on his hips, staring with frustration at Rafe. "So you're not going to change clothes and go with us?"

Crossing over to the bed, Rafe picked up his belt and began to thread it through the loops on his jeans. "I wouldn't trade a date with Lilly for any ball."

"So you're getting serious about the woman?"

Glancing up, Rafe sneered at his brother. "Serious? Why does that word always have to come up when a woman is the subject of the conversation? What does it mean, anyway? Do I want to marry her? Well, if that's what you're asking, then no. I'm not going to marry her. I'm not ever going to marry any woman! Is that plain enough for you?"

"You're sickening. You really are," Clancy muttered then quickly started toward the door. "I'll explain to Dad that you have other responsibilities tonight. I'm sure he'll understand."

"Sure, Clancy. Give me that indignant act—I don't care. 'Cause I sure as hell don't see you taking a wife or even trying to find one. So get off my back about Lilly!"

Clancy didn't make any sort of reply. Instead, he quietly shut the door behind him.

Once his brother was out of sight, Rafe grabbed up his hat, crammed it on his head and started toward the door, but halfway there he caught himself and slowly returned to the bed. Sinking onto the edge of the mattress, he wiped a hand over his face and drew in a long, calming breath.

First Finn and now Clancy, he thought ruefully. He'd just behaved like a complete jerk. Sure, he'd always had a short fuse, but it wasn't like him to fly off the handle like this. So what was gnawing at him?

His job had always required long, tiring hours in the saddle with plenty of stress and worry to go along with them. But in spite of that he loved it and the ranch. And having a woman like Lilly in his life would make any man a happy guy. Besides giving him red-hot sex, she also understood him and was instinctively attuned to his thoughts and dreams and wishes. He had an incredible woman. Or did he? What did *have* really mean? For the present? For a few more weeks or months?

A few nights ago when he'd taken Lilly to the Sierra Chateau for dinner and dancing, a young man she was acquainted with had stopped by their table and invited her to dance. And even though she'd politely declined, the incident had opened Rafe's eyes. Suddenly, he was seeing that Lilly wasn't his wife. She didn't belong solely to him. She had a right to go out with another man. She even had a right to feed him sandwiches in bed and then make red-hot love to him. The same as she'd done to Rafe. The whole idea revolted him. But the idea of marriage was just as troubling.

He wasn't going to think about what tomorrow was going to bring, he told himself as he rose to his feet and snatched his wallet from the dresser top. He had more blessings than he could count. And tonight he was going to do his best to remember that.

A half hour later, when Lilly opened the door and welcomed Rafe into the house, he forgot all about the testy exchange with Clancy and the fact that he was missing the cattleman's ball, an event he'd attended every year since he was eighteen years old.

"Something smells delicious," he said as he pulled off his hat and placed it on a wall table near the door. "I'm not sure if it's you or the dinner."

Smiling impishly, she stepped forward and slipped her arms around his waist. "I hope it's the dinner. Cooking a meal is much harder than dabbing on perfume."

Bending his head, he kissed her lips and a sweet rush of familiarity struck him hard, reminding him that she was the only woman he'd ever wanted this much for this long.

"You shouldn't have gone to so much trouble. We could've had pizza or something delivered."

"I invited you to dinner, remember? I wanted to prepare you a meal. It probably won't be up to Greta's standards, but I promise it will be edible." She eased out of his arms and motioned for him to follow her to the kitchen. "Come sit while I finish everything. Would you like a drink? The only thing I have with alcohol in it is beer. Or I have ginger ale or fruit punch."

"I'm fine. I'll just wait until we eat."

As he followed her out of the living room, Rafe could hardly ignore the sway of her hips beneath the floral skirt she was wearing and the way her golden-blond hair tumbled around her shoulders. If he had it his way, he'd grab her up right now and carry her to the bedroom. But it was obvious that she'd gone to a lot of trouble to prepare him this meal. He wasn't about to ruin it for any reason.

Inside the kitchen, she'd already set the table with large, bottle-green plates, heavy silverware and an array of condiments. Instead of taking a seat there, he followed her over to the cabinet counter and sidled as close to her as he could without hindering her movement.

"As soon as I finish this salad everything will be ready," she told him as she picked up a wedge of lettuce and began tearing it into a wooden bowl. "Are you hungry?"

"Very. We ate sandwiches out on the trail about eleven this morning. I've not eaten since."

"And did you get all the calves rounded up safely?"

It thrilled him that she paid attention to his work and remembered what he was doing for the day. Was that what having a wife meant? he wondered. Having a woman around who actually cared about his life?

*I'm not ever going to marry any woman! Is that plain enough for you?*

The words he'd barked at Clancy continued to roll around in his head and reminded him that Lilly didn't have to be his wife in order for her to care about his work or what went on in his life. She already cared. That was enough for him. But would she care years from now? Or would she move on to a man who would give her a home and babies?

Trying to push aside his battling thoughts, he said, "It took longer than I'd planned, and one of the men took a tumble when his horse ran him under a tree limb. Thankfully, he wasn't hurt. And all the calves are branded and vaccinated now."

She dumped pieces of tomato and cucumber over the lettuce then began to toss the simple salad with a large fork and spoon. "I thought about you riding in the mountains. You're going to have to show me more of the ranch soon. Whenever we can work around our schedules. If

I ever expect to keep up with you, I need to get my riding legs in shape."

He chuckled lowly. "As far as I can see your legs are in perfect shape."

She pulled a playful face at him. "There are two glasses in the freezer already filled with ice. Would you mind putting them on the table while I get the food?"

"I can do that." As he fetched the glasses, he said, "I did happen to come upon a beautiful spot today over by Eagle's Ridge that I'd like to share with you."

"Oh, tell me about it."

"No way. I want it to be a surprise."

She carried a large casserole dish over to the table and placed it on a hot pad. "Then I'll have to trust you when you say it's beautiful."

Snaring an arm around her waist, he pulled her close enough to press a light kiss on her lips. "Not nearly as beautiful as you, Lilly. You're tempting me something awful, you know it?"

Laughing, she pushed him lightly into the seat at the end of the oval table. "You'll survive."

He stayed put while she placed the rest of the food on the table and filled their glasses with water. When she finally took the seat angled to the right of him, he reached over and clasped her hand in his. "Thank you, Lilly, for going to all this trouble for me. I can't tell you how much I've missed you these past few days."

Her smile was tender and the sight of it smoothed all the rough edges he'd been feeling since Clancy had come to his room.

She said lowly, "And I've missed you, too, Rafe."

He rubbed his thumb across the back of her hand. "The cattlemen's ball is going on tonight. Clancy was put out with me because I didn't go. It's the first one I've missed since I was eighteen."

"Oh, Rafe, I hope I wasn't the reason," she exclaimed. "We could've done this another night."

"I'd already made this date with you. And I wasn't going to break it for anything. But if someone had reminded me that the ball was coming up, I would've invited you to go with me. It's a fancy bash. Everyone gets dressed up and steaks are served for dinner. There'll be live music and lots of dancing. You might have enjoyed it."

She began to laugh and he frowned with confusion.

"What's funny about that?"

She gestured toward the casserole dish. "You're going to be disappointed. You could have enjoyed a juicy steak. Instead, you're getting chicken and rice.

He slanted her a sly look. "I'll take a plate of chicken and an evening with you over anything."

"I'll remind you of that when we start to wash the dishes," she teased.

After that they began to eat, and for the next half hour Rafe learned exactly how good Lilly could cook. By the time he finished a piece of the German chocolate cake she'd made for dessert, he was completely stuffed.

"More cake or coffee?" she asked as she pushed aside her plate.

"Everything was delicious, Lilly. But all I want now is you."

"Rafe, you—I want to—"

Before she could say more he wrapped a hand around her wrist and tugged her out of her chair and onto his lap.

With her head cradled in the crook of his arm, he gazed down at her. "Go to bed with me. Right?"

A strange, wistful look came into her eyes and for a moment he thought she was going to wriggle off his lap and refuse. But then she suddenly groaned and wrapped her arms around his neck.

Rafe didn't waste time pondering her hesitation. He carried her straight to the bedroom and by the time he'd peeled away her clothing, her mouth was clinging hotly to his, her hands clutching him close. And the troubled shadows he saw in her eyes back in the kitchen were completely forgotten.

## Chapter Ten

More than an hour later, Lilly lay cuddled in the curve of Rafe's warm body. His cheek was pressed against the top of her head, while his fingers were meandering from her hair to the bare slope of her arm.

Being next to him in the quiet of the bedroom, her body replete from his lovemaking, she should've been feeling happy and perfect. Instead, she could only wonder how soon it would be before everything between them ended.

"You've been quiet this evening, Lilly. Tell me what's wrong."

The tenderness in his voice caused her heart to wince, and for a moment she hesitated to answer. Maybe it would be best if she shoved all her desires and wants aside? Maybe having him like this for a brief time was better than to risk losing him completely? But she had to think about her future now, because Rafe surely wasn't.

Her throat was suddenly aching from the lump that had gathered there, making her voice hoarse when she finally said, "I don't think you really want me to tell you."

Lifting his head, he looked down at her. "If something is on your mind, Lilly, I want to hear it. I don't want things to be hidden between us."

She turned in his arms and brought her hand up to his cheek. "Do you have any idea how much I care for you, Rafe? Really?"

He went still and Lilly could feel his body tightening, bracing as though he was dreading what was coming next.

He said in a guarded tone, "I think you like me. And I think you want me. Otherwise, I wouldn't be here in your bed."

The only reason that Rafe was in her bed was because she loved him. Maybe deep down Lilly had known that all along. But she'd wanted to pretend that her heart hadn't been involved. Now she'd slowly and surely come to the realization that she couldn't pretend anymore.

"That's true," she said. "I do like you and want you. But something has happened to me and—"

She broke off and as she searched for the right words to say, his gaze delved deeper into hers.

"You've met someone else. Is that what you're trying to tell me?"

She'd not expected him to be thinking along those terms and his question totally threw her off balance.

"No! That's not what I meant." Groaning with frustration, she rolled away from him and sat up on the edge of the bed. As she reached for her robe draped over the footboard, she said, "All right, I'm just going to come out and say it. I don't think—I can't go on like this."

"What do you mean by—*this?*"

He sounded annoyed, but Lilly had expected that.

Pulling on her robe, she looked over her shoulder at him. "Rafe, I understand that we made a deal. Nothing serious. No strings. And I truly believed that's what I wanted. But I never expected this thing between us to go this long or get this involved."

Swinging his legs over the side of the bed, he reached for his shorts and jeans. "So what are you wanting, Lilly? To end it? Not more than an hour ago we were talking about taking a ride in the mountains. I don't know where all of this is coming from or why."

Walking around the end of the bed, she went to stand in front of him. "I don't want it to end, Rafe. But I've figured out that I'm more old-fashioned than I thought. Just having an affair is not what I want for myself. And I understand that you don't want anything more serious than that. So that doesn't leave us with much of a future, does it?"

He stood up and after zipping and buttoning his jeans, he looked at her. Lilly couldn't help but notice that his jaw was tight, his lips pressed to a thin line. But then she'd hardly expected smiles or even a look of understanding from the man.

"Tonight, tomorrow, that's our future, Lilly. Not weeks or months from now. Hell, we don't even know if we'll be alive in another year."

Amazed by his cynical outlook, she folded her arms over her breasts and stared at him. "You don't have to remind me how fragile life is, Rafe. In my line of work I see death all too often. But I'm not letting it dictate my thoughts or plans."

He collected his shirt from the floor and jammed his

arms into the sleeves. "I'm not dwelling on death, Lilly," he said in a tired voice. "Nor do I need a therapist to un-ravel my hang-ups. I just need for you to keep your end of our bargain. Nothing serious. No strings. Only the pleasure of each other's company. Remember?"

Her face was suddenly burning with anger and hu-miliation. She'd been wrong, she thought, so wrong to give herself to a man who wanted nothing more from her than her body. Why hadn't she realized that from the very beginning?

*Because you thought you could keep your heart all wrapped up in a safe little cocoon. You believed that being with Rafe was simply going to bring some pleasure into your life. Not love.*

Flustered by her thoughts, she muttered flatly, "I shouldn't have ever said that. I made a mistake in think-ing I could just hang around and be your woman until you grew tired of me."

Snapping the front of his shirt together, he closed the short space between them. "Lilly, I've never misled you at any time about my intentions, have I?"

His words were like fist blows to her chest, making it difficult to breathe past the pain. "No. You made it quite clear you're not a marrying man. Yet these past few weeks you've wanted to get all the benefits of a husband without making a commitment."

Even in the dim lighting of the bedroom she could see his face turn pale. "You seemed to be enjoying it," he said accusingly.

Lilly lifted her chin. "I still enjoy being with you, Rafe," she said softly. "But I'd like to know that I'm more than just a pastime for you. That you'd like to have me around not just for sex for a few weeks or months, but for a lifetime of love, as well."

He raked a hand through his hair then shook his head. "Apparently, you've changed, Lilly. But don't expect me to change with you. Don't try to turn me into something other than what I am. I'm not a family man. I never will be."

Turning her back to him, she squeezed her eyes shut and willed the pain in her chest to go away. Thank God she'd not told him exactly how much she loved him. At least she could save herself a little pride.

"That's your choice, Rafe. Just like it's my choice to want something else out of life." Turning back to him, she let out a long, soulful breath. "For a long time after Grant dumped me, I could hardly stand to look at a man—any man. And for all these years since, I believed that my chance to have a husband and children was over. Like a fool, I thought that everything had ended because of him. But being with you has opened my eyes, Rafe. It's made me realize how much time I've wasted and all the things I truly want for myself."

Turning away from her, he grabbed up his boots. As he jerked them on, he asked sarcastically, "And what if I say I'll marry you, Lilly? Would you believe I was sincere? Would you trust me to put all other women aside? Considering my reputation, I somehow doubt it."

She felt sick. The deep-down kind of sick that no medication would help. "I've never thought you were a dishonest person, Rafe. You wouldn't be here in my bedroom if I believed anything less. And if you were man enough to make a commitment to me, then yes, I would believe you meant it."

Straightening to his full height, he looked at her and

for one brief moment there was a torn look in his eyes, but just as quickly it was replaced with fierce independence. "I thought you were going to be different, Lilly. I believed you would respect my views and wishes. Now you want to hog-tie me—"

"No, Rafe," she interrupted. "I have no intentions of tying you any which way. I—"

Before she could get another word out, he took her by the shoulders and pulled her into his arms.

"Oh, Lilly, why are you doing this to us?" he asked, his soft voice filled with anguish. "Things were going along so good. Why can't we keep things just as they are?"

Tears clawed at her eyes and she desperately blinked them away. "Rafe, you just made it very clear that you don't want anything permanent with me. I went through that once. I—"

His fingers tightened on her shoulders. "I'm not that intern. I'm not lying to you—feeding you a line about marriage just to keep you in my bed. Why—"

She was going to have to tear herself open, she thought dismally, and let him see everything. Otherwise, he might never understand how she felt about herself or him and the future.

Pulling away from him, she walked around to the end of the bed and braced her hands on the footboard. "That's not the only thing I went through with Grant. His deceit was the easiest part to get over. The rest I—"

"Go on," he prompted. "What about the rest?"

She took a deep breath and though it would have been easier to look away from him, she didn't. She wanted him to see the pain in her eyes. Then maybe, just maybe, his heart might begin to see.

"I got pregnant with Grant's child. When I told him

about the baby he was furious and demanded that I get an abortion. As an intern just starting his career, he couldn't afford to pay child support to an unwanted child. Not to mention that when the rumor of my pregnancy got around it would put a cramp in his philandering. I refused to end the pregnancy, but that was hardly the reason Grant high-tailed it out of my life. He'd never had any intentions of sticking around for very long."

His features were stark and unmoving as his gaze swept over her face. "So what happened?"

Unwittingly, her fingers clenched the wooden foot-board. "I was heading into my fourth month when I suffered a miscarriage."

A muscle jumped in his jaw and she wondered what he was thinking. Disgust? Empathy? Or dear God, perhaps he was indifferent to the loss she'd endured.

"Oh."

She released a pent-up breath. "That was during the time I became friends with your mother. She's the only person who ever knew about the baby. If I hadn't had her support I think I would have crumbled emotionally."

She could see his throat working as he swallowed and the reaction told her that, at least, he was affected by something she'd said. Most likely the mention of his mother, she thought sadly.

"What about your own parents—your mother? You didn't let them know what you were going through?"

Shaking her head, she walked back to where he continued to stand by the side of the bed. "Against my father's wishes, I left home when I was eighteen. You see, the environment in my parents' home wasn't really family at all. It was constant hell. I wanted out of it, so I left, went to work and took care of myself. My mom never was the nurturing, mothering sort. And my dad—well, he'd suffered enough disappointment and heartache without learning that his daughter had made a huge fool of herself. I was determined to handle my own problems by myself."

"So my mom—what sort of advice did she give you?"

"Mostly that I was strong and young and healthy and that someday I'd find a wonderful man who would love me and want me to have his children. I have to hold on to her guidance, Rafe. Even if you can't be that man."

Lifting his face toward the ceiling, he groaned. "So you've broken your promise about not getting serious. You've changed your mind about wanting a husband and children. And I'm not supposed to feel used or angry," he said tightly. "Well, I realize that you have the right to change your mind, but right now I'm feeling like a damned idiot for trusting you to keep your part of our bargain."

Anger spurted through her. "Well, excuse me for being a woman, Mr. Calhoun!"

His head jerked around and this time his eyes were boring into hers. "Damn it, Lilly, you're trying to steamroll me into being something other than what I am. I don't allow my men to bulldoze me and the same goes for women. Including you!"

Stunned by his callousness, Lilly pointed to the door. "If that's all you have to say to me, then get the hell out! And don't come back!"

"Gladly."

Lilly watched him stalk out of the room, then moments later the front door slammed shut. The finality of the sound shook her from the spot where she'd been standing and she walked out to the kitchen where the leftovers from their dinner still sat on the table.

Rafe had escaped helping her clean the kitchen, she thought grimly. But she'd escaped much more. Like letting herself hold on to any sort of hope that Rafe could ever love her.

For the next two weeks, the June weather turned dry and extremely hot, scorching every blade of grass on the lower ranges of the Silver Horn. To save on hay cost, Rafe and the men had been driving several of the herds to higher mountain slopes, where the cooler temperatures had kept most of the grass from burning.

When he and the crew finally rode into the ranch yard, after spending twelve hours in the saddle, horses and men were both dragging and Rafe was hardly in the mood for whining.

When Denver approached him in the saddling paddock, he did his best to listen patiently to his request to allow three of the men to take the next day off. But once the ramrod finished speaking, Rafe practically shouted, "I'd sure as hell like a day off, too, Denver. But we still have at least a thousand head of cattle to move yet. The weather is forecast to get even hotter in the next three days. The cattle can't wait around while the men take a vacation!"

"None of them is asking for a vacation, Rafe. Each of them has personal issues to deal with. Surely you can understand that."

"I said no! If they don't want to show up for work then they can take their wrangling to another ranch. And if you don't want to tell them that, then I sure as hell can!"

Rafe lifted the heavy saddle off Roscoe's back and

heaved it onto the top rail of the fence. Behind him, the tall, dark ramrod shook his head.

"I don't know what's wrong with you, Rafe, but I'm telling you now, you'd better get your act together or you're not going to have any men to give orders to."

Rafe whirled around to remind the ramrod he'd soon be out of a paycheck if he kept on, but Denver was already striding away to the opposite side of the small paddock.

Hellfire! What was the matter with his men? They'd worked long, hot days before. They had enough sense to know this wasn't the time to be asking for days off.

*You need to be asking what's wrong with yourself, Rafe. You ought to be remembering that your men have feelings, too. They want to be treated with the same respect that you expect.*

The voice going off in Rafe's head was his own conscience and it had him grunting cynically and turning back to Roscoe. As he lifted the wet blankets and pad from the horse's back, Lilly's image swam in front of him. For a moment he stared off in space and let himself remember the incredible pleasure of kissing her, touching every part of her, making love to her.

*Making love.* Was that what he'd been doing all those nights with Lilly? After these past two weeks without her, he'd been doing plenty of thinking. He could now admit that his connection to her had been much more than sexual gratification. But love? What did he know about that fleeting emotion? Next to nothing.

Down through the years, Rafe had never given himself the chance or the time with any woman to feel more than momentary pleasure. And he'd not expected anything to be different with Lilly. But something had happened to him from the first moment he'd laid eyes on her. The more time he'd spent with her, the more he'd wanted to be with her. Now he was lost and miserable.

That fact had been more than apparent to him yesterday when he'd walked into a diner in Carson City and spotted an old girlfriend sitting at the back of the room. Any other time he would've made a beeline to her table and charmed her into a date. Instead, he'd deliberately ignored her, even when she'd waved for him to join her. He'd not wanted to even talk to her, much less go out with her. He didn't want any woman but Lilly.

But the way he saw it, there was nothing he could do about changing the situation. Lilly had made her choice. She wanted a ring on her finger, a baby in her arms and a husband to grow old with. Well, that wasn't him. No. He wasn't about to be roped into all that responsibility and the restrictions it would put on his life. Even more, he wasn't going to invest his heart and soul into someone and then have them ripped away for one reason or another.

From this point on he was going to forget about women. Period. His work was his life and that was the way he was going to keep it.

Shaking his head in an effort to rid himself of the miserable thought, he stroked Roscoe's neck. "Come on, boy. Let's go to the barn and I'll brush you down and get your supper."

The long white barn where Rafe kept Roscoe stalled was a good fifty yards away, and as the horse plodded tiredly behind him, he glanced up, his gaze taking him far beyond the busy ranch yard to the mountains in the distance.

He'd planned to take Lilly riding to that beautiful spot near Eagle's Ridge but that would never happen now, he thought soberly. His time with her had ended and he needed to forget her. Trouble was, he hadn't figured out how to do that yet.

The next morning Lilly was walking slowly next to Bart as the two of them carefully made their way across the upper-floor balcony. Using only her arm as a balancing tool, Bart was taking longer, more confident steps than he'd ever managed before and Lilly couldn't have been more proud of his progress.

"At this rate, Bart, you're going to be dancing soon," she told him.

He let out a hearty chuckle. "That would be the day! I haven't danced in years. Not since Gilda and I were young."

"Then you ought to try it," Lilly suggested. "It would be good for your leg and your spirits."

"Well, now, if you'd go with me, Lilly, I just might try it. A steak dinner and dancing with a beautiful blonde afterwards. I could handle that."

"I could handle it, too," she agreed with a little laugh. "But the gossips would sure have a field day about us."

"Bah! People have always talked about me. Might as well give them something to really work their jaws," he said.

By now they were getting close to the open door of Bart's study, and Lilly purposely tugged him to a stop. "I think we've made enough rounds this morning. Think you can make it back to your chair on your own? I'm going down to the kitchen to see if Greta will fix us some coffee."

"I'm on my way," he assured her. "And while you're

at it, see if the old woman has any of those cinnamon rolls left."

"Think you deserve one?" Lilly asked impishly.

He winked at her. "I think we both deserve one."

"I'll ask," Lilly promised, then hurried across the landing toward the staircase.

The moment she put her hand on the balustrade and took one step downward, she sensed someone's presence and glanced up to see Rafe standing halfway up the staircase. Like the morning she first laid eyes on him, he was dressed all in cowboy rig with his scarred chaps riding low on his hips and his black hat slanted rakishly over one eye. The sleeves of his white shirt were rolled back against his forearms and the sight of the corded muscles was an instant reminder of how it felt to be encircled and cradled by all that strength.

"Hello, Rafe," she said, her voice low and thick. "What are you doing here?"

His lips twisted to a sardonic line. "I live here. Remember?"

His cutting attitude instantly stiffened her spine as she descended several steps toward him. "Sure. I remember. But this isn't your normal hangout at this time of the morning."

"I was on my way up to see Dad. Not you."

She flinched inside but on the outside she managed to keep her expression stoic. This man didn't need her. He only needed himself. She had to remember that.

"I never imagined that you were," she said stiffly. "Now if you'll excuse me, I'm on my way to the kitchen."

"Yes, I heard. For coffee and cinnamon rolls." The look he was giving her was nothing less than a sneer. "Just exactly what are you doing, Lilly?"

Her brows shot up as she tried to decipher the meaning of his question. "Doing? I've been giving your grandfather his morning therapy session. Now we're finished and we're going to enjoy a bit of a break before I leave for the day. Not that it's any of your business," she clipped.

"Really? Well, I heard that little exchange between you and my grandfather. What's going on with you, Lilly? Just because you can't get your hooks in me, you've turned your claws toward my grandfather? If I thought for one minute—"

Outraged, she interrupted. "You were eavesdropping on our conversation? You're sick, Rafe! In more ways than one!"

"I heard you agree to go on a date with the old man!" he accused.

"So what? It sure as heck isn't any of your business who I go out with. And that includes Bart."

"Why, you little money-grubbing—"

She wasn't about to let him finish. She cracked her palm hard against his jaw. "Get away from me, you monster!"

Taking advantage of his stunned reaction, she started to shoot past him, but he instantly grabbed her by the arm and jerked her back to him. The sudden movement rocked her off balance and caused her to nearly topple forward.

Snatching a grip on both her shoulders, he pulled her safely to him and for a moment he simply held her. Above her head, Lilly could hear his harsh breathing and beneath her cheek his heart was pounding wildly. She didn't know what he was thinking, but she knew she had to get away from him and quick. Otherwise, she'd be throwing her pride aside.

Prying her hands between them, she pushed at his

chest. "You can let me go now," she said between gritted teeth.

"What if I don't want to?"

Darting a glance up at him, she opened her mouth to reply, but he didn't give her the chance. Instead, his head swooped down and the next thing she knew he was kissing her with hungry persuasion. Lilly couldn't push him away. Not when every cell in her body was crying to hold on to him and never let go. But thankfully after a moment he lifted his head and sanity rushed in to gather her scattered senses.

"Oh, Lilly," he said in a tortured whisper. "This rift between us is killing me!"

"Take two aspirins and put your feet up. You'll get over it."

Ignoring his shocked expression, she jerked away from him and hurried on down the stairs. Behind her, she could hear the clank of his spurs, but she didn't allow herself to look over her shoulder to see if he was coming after her or going on up the stairs. One way or the other, she couldn't let herself care anymore.

## Chapter Eleven

Three days later, Lilly and Marcella met in the hospital to have lunch together before their shift began. As they ate, Marcella caught her up on the progress Jett Sundell had made in her effort to adopt Peter.

"Mr. Sundell is a father, you know, so I think he understands what adopting Peter means to me. He's been working hard on my case. If things go as planned, in the next few days I'll be taking Peter home as my foster son. And hopefully, later on, a complete adoption will happen."

It was good to see the smile on her friend's face. Marcella had been through a few tough years. She deserved some happiness in her life. "Marcella, that's great news. I'm so happy for you."

From across the table, Marcella cast her a skeptical glance. "Are you, really? When I first talked to you about Peter, you didn't seem all that keen on the idea."

Lilly waved a dismissive hand at her. "I hadn't had

time to think—I was only concerned about you raising two boys alone. Now that I have thought it through, I believe it will be a good thing for you, Harry and Peter. Besides, you're not always going to be a single mother. Some man is going to come along and snatch you up."

"Hah! If I can't find one who wants a divorcée with one child, how do you expect me to find one willing to take on a divorced woman with two children?"

"It would take a special man, all right," Lilly admitted. "But he's out there somewhere. You'll find him."

"Sure. I'll have to find him on a gurney. Delirious with fever," Marcella said with a laugh, then slanted a pointed look at Lilly. "We've not had much time to talk these past few days. I'm curious to know what's going on with Mr. Calhoun."

"You mean Bart? He's coming along wonderfully. In fact, my job with him will be finished soon. And I'm—well, I'm feeling torn about that."

"How so?"

Lilly shrugged as her gaze dropped to the partially eaten salad on her plate. "I'm very happy that Bart has recovered so nicely. His mobility is back to eighty or more percent—a miracle after the shape he was initially in after the stroke."

"I'd be feeling pretty proud of myself and him."

Lilly sighed. "I am. But I'm going to miss him terribly. You know, everyone warned me that he was going to be a terror. Instead, I've grown very fond of him. And I think he feels the same way about me."

Marcella studied her closely. "Actually, I wasn't talking about Bart. I want to know about Rafe."

Just the mention of the man's name was enough to send a chill rushing over Lilly. "I couldn't tell you anything about Rafe," she said stiffly. "Other than I never plan to see the man again."

Marcella's mouth flopped open. "Lilly! What—oh, damn, my phone is vibrating. I'd better see who's calling." She pulled the device from a pocket on her uniform and after a quick glance pushed her chair back from the table. "Sorry, Lilly, would you hate me for cutting lunch short? It's Mom and I need to talk to her in private—my brother is having some serious problems and—"

"Don't apologize. You go on," Lilly assured her. "I'll meet you back in emergency."

With a grateful smile, Marcella hurried away and Lilly tried to turn her attention back to her meal, but now that Marcella had brought up the subject of Rafe Calhoun, her stomach wasn't in the mood.

Running into him on the staircase the other day had been bittersweet. She couldn't deny that she missed him terribly, or that being in his arms, even for those few seconds had been precious. But he'd made it clear how he felt about her. No plans or promises. Enjoy today because there probably wouldn't be a tomorrow. Well, she couldn't live like that. Not anymore. Now she realized exactly how much she needed someone to share her life with. How much she wanted a husband and children. It would probably take her a long time to get over Rafe and finally find a man she could love. Especially one who would want to settle down and make a family with her. But she wasn't going to give up and settle for less.

"I see you lost your lunch partner. Mind if I sit down until she's back?"

The male voice jerked Lilly out of her melancholy thoughts and she glanced up to see Chet Anderson standing at the side of the small round table.

"Hello, Chet. Please join me. Marcella won't be back."

He eased into the chair that Marcella had just vacated and pushed the plate with a half-eaten sandwich aside. Since he didn't have a lunch tray with him, Lilly asked, "Aren't you going to eat?"

He grimaced. "I'm actually on my way to a business luncheon across town. But as I walked by I spotted you here and wanted to say hello. How are things going with Doctor Sherman?"

Lilly smiled ruefully. "No more problems, thank goodness. Actually, he's seemed a little subdued since that confrontation."

Chet shook his head with misgivings. "I'm trying to keep an open mind about the man, Lilly. He's not from this area and who knows what's been going on in his private life. I'm hoping he'll pull it all together and become a respected doctor on the hospital staff."

Lilly thoughtfully used her straw to stir the sugar in the bottom of her tea glass. "Yeah, well, we all have our problems, but that doesn't mean we can take them to work with us."

As miserable as she'd been these past few weeks without Rafe in her life, she'd done her best not to let it interfere with her work. When another's health was involved, she didn't have the luxury to dwell on her own personal feelings. And that was a good thing. Because the thought of never making love to Rafe again was like never seeing the sun or the stars again. But she'd get over it. She had to.

"So is that man of yours still making you happy?" Chet inquired.

Glancing across the room, Lilly stared unseeingly at the people passing through the cafeteria line. "I'm not seeing him anymore," she said bluntly.

Clearly surprised, he said, "Oh. Well, I'm sorry." As soon as the words were out, he shook his head. "No. That's not true. I'm glad. Maybe now you'll think about having dinner with me one night soon."

And why not, Lilly asked herself. Chet was the complete opposite of Rafe. He wasn't obscenely rich or from ranching royalty. He wasn't a playboy or a rakish rascal. He was the steady, predictable sort. Yet he didn't make her heart beat fast or her body ache with longing. And perhaps that was a good thing, she thought dismally. Wouldn't a long, practical marriage be better than a brief, passionate affair?

"I can only promise that I'll think about it," she said solemnly. She tried to give him a smile, but from the look on his face, she wasn't fooling him any more than she was herself.

"Lilly, as much as I'd like a chance with you, if this guy really means that much to you—then maybe you should try—"

"There's nothing to try," she cut in. "We have different ideas about things."

He reached across the table and covered her hand with his, but unlike Rafe's, the touch was like that of a comforting friend. "You know where to find me if you need to talk. Or if you need anything at all."

She nodded. "Thanks, Chet."

"See you later."

He left the table and though Lilly watched him walk away, all she could see was Rafe.

Later that same afternoon, Rafe was at the vet barn, looking on while the doctor treated a bull with an infected horn when his father walked up beside him. The sight of Orin in the vet barn was highly unusual and took Rafe by surprise.

Since Rafe's mother had died, his father had abruptly quit all outside work and started behaving as though he was too old to endure the rigor of wrangling. He'd turned his favorite horse out to pasture, hung up his spurs and now spent his days indoors doing paperwork or traveling on business matters.

Rafe had missed the camaraderie of working side by side with his father and as a result he'd felt as though his mother's death had ultimately caused him to lose his father, too.

"Hey, Dad, what brings you down here? I thought you were going to Ely today to look at some cattle."

From the stern look on Orin's face, Rafe supposed it would be foolish to hope this unexpected visit from his father meant he was finally returning to the man he used to be.

"I had planned to already be on my way," Orin said, his voice clipped. "But I've had a few distractions this morning."

Now what? Rafe wondered miserably. Ever since he'd walked out of Lilly's house, everything on the ranch had seemed to go sour, and though he kept telling himself he'd get over this wretchedness he was feeling, each day that passed without her only seemed to make it worse.

"What kind of distractions?" Rafe made himself ask.

Orin jerked his head toward the open doorway behind them. "Let's go to my truck. I need to talk with you."

Rafe was thirty years old and had worked as the Silver Horn foreman for the past five of those. He was a grown man and yet his father still had a tendency to order him around as though he was a little boy. The fact irked him, but he tried his best not to show it.

"Denver is meeting me over at the horse barn in ten minutes," he explained to his father.

"This won't take that long," he said briskly, then turned and strode away, fully confident that Rafe would follow.

Taking a deep, bracing breath, Rafe took one last glance at the bull, then took off after Orin.

Outside, the sun was fierce with only a stray cloud here and there to offer any sort of relief from the heat. By the time Rafe reached his father's diesel truck, Orin was already perched beneath the steering wheel. The windows were up and the motor idling.

Rafe climbed inside and shut the door to keep the cold, air-conditioned air trapped inside the cab. "Okay. I'm here. What's going on?"

Orin stared straight ahead. "You fired James, Shane and Jeb for asking for a day off. I—"

"That's right," Rafe butted in. "They all three knew what was going on at the time and—"

"I don't need to hear the details, Rafe! I just thought you ought to know I've hired them back. And you—"

Boiling blood instantly shot to the top of Rafe's head. "Hired them back! Damn it all, how am I supposed to demand any respect from my men if you undermine me like this?"

Orin leveled a black stare at his son. "Respect? Let me tell you, son, the way you've been behaving, you're not going to get anything from the men. Not even any work. I had to practically beg those three to come back. And half of the remaining crew are threatening to walk off."

Rafe felt like his father had reached across the console and gave him a hard whack on the side of the head. "Walk off? What are you talking about?"

Orin shook his head with disbelief. "You didn't know, did you? But that's not surprising. Denver tells me the men can't talk to you anymore. He says you've changed and that you're either biting their heads off or giving them unreasonable orders."

Denver had been his right-hand man for as long as Rafe had been foreman. To hear that the other man had gone over his head and spoken to Orin about this problem was like a kick in the gut to Rafe. Did he actually deserve this? Sure, he'd been driving the men a little hard, but not any more than he'd been driving himself.

"So he—" The furious words on the tip of Rafe's tongue suddenly died as a lost, lonely feeling swept through him. Was there anyone that even gave a damn that his whole world was crashing in on him?

*No one knows your world is crumbling, Rafe. You've been going around hiding your pain behind a wall of anger. You have too much pride to admit to anyone that Lilly has walked out of your life. That you weren't man enough to hold on to her.*

"Sounds like everyone thinks I'm one big mess-up," he said dourly.

Disgust marred Orin's dark features. "That's one way of putting it."

Rafe groaned. "Look, Dad, everything I do is for the ranch. The heat has played hell with the grass. The cattle are my first priority. It's not like I enjoy laying the law down to the men. But things have to get done."

Orin's nostrils flared and Rafe couldn't remember the last time he'd seen his father this upset with him. Probably not since Rafe had been a teenager. Which only made this tête-à-tête even more humiliating.

"At what cost, Rafe? The men who work this ranch are more than just machines! They have personal lives, too. They have their own issues to deal with—just like you do. You've been so wrapped up in yourself that you seem to have forgotten that. I'm going to be damned frank, son. You either get your head on straight or I'm going to step in and take over for you."

Rafe stared in wonder at his father, while his mind tried to picture his life as something other than the Horn foreman. With Lilly gone, the ranch was the only thing he had left to push him forward. Now he was in jeopardy of losing it.

"Listen, Dad, I'll admit that I might have jumped the gun with those three firings. But I've not ever asked the men to work any harder or put in more hours than I do myself. As for you—I'm not sure that you—" He broke off abruptly as he realized there wasn't any kind way of telling his father that the daily rigors of the foreman job would be too much physical stress for him to handle.

Orin scowled at him. "That I can hold up to long hours in the saddle anymore? If that's what you were about to say, then you'd better think again, Rafe! I'm not ancient," he muttered, then added under his breath, "Although you boys probably think I am. And that's my own fault. But things are going to change around here."

Rattled by Orin's forewarnings, he searched his father's face. Had Rafe been so wrapped up in himself that he'd not noticed how his father was changing? Had losing Lilly blinded him that much?

"What does that mean?" Rafe asked him.

Orin's jaw remained tight. "The fact is—I'm not happy with you or myself."

Rafe heaved out a heavy breath. It was already bad enough that he'd lost Lilly and alienated his men. Being at loggerheads with his father would pretty much paint the rest of his sky black.

"Don't worry, Dad. I'll make it right with the men. There's no need for you to drag out your spurs or put in long hours with the crew."

Orin's heavy sigh was full of resignation. "This isn't all about keeping a rein on you, Rafe. Even though you've been behaving like a jackass, I happen to believe you're going to get your head on straight—eventually. I'm going to trust you to keep the men happy and working. I'm thinking in the long-term now—I need to get my thumb back on the pulse of the ranch again—for a lot of reasons."

Rafe wasn't exactly sure what his father meant by that. But he couldn't help but feel a spurt of hope. For so long he'd prayed to see his father back in the saddle and enjoying the ranch as he had before Claudia died.

"Does this mean you're actually going to get out of the damned house and start wrangling again?"

The other man opened his mouth to reply, then deciding against it, he shook his head. "I don't want to get into all of that now. We'll discuss it when I get back from Ely. I'll be staying the night there and return late tomorrow evening."

"Fine. I'll see you when you get back." Rafe opened the door to climb out of the truck. "Have a safe trip, Dad."

"Rafe."

Standing on the ground now, Rafe looked back into the truck cab at his father. "Was there something else?"

"Just remember you have to show some loyalty. Without loyalty you don't have much at all."

Nodding, Rafe shut the truck door between them then thoughtfully watched his father drive away.

*Loyalty.* The word churned in his mind as he stared across the dusty ranch yard. It was the thing Lilly had wanted and needed from him. She deserved it from him. But he'd been unable to give it to her. And now, like his father had just said, Rafe didn't have much of anything.

Pulling himself back to the present, he started toward the horse barn and as he went his gaze instinctively drifted over to the big house. Three days ago, when he'd encountered Lilly on the stairs, the meeting had in many ways been déjà vu for Rafe. The pleasurable memories of first meeting her there had been mangled with the anger and hurt that had been boiling in him ever since she'd ordered him out of her house. And then suddenly she'd teetered on the step and most likely would've fallen if he'd not caught her. Just thinking about it now sent shivers of fear down his spine. Lilly could have suffered the same fate as his mother. In that instant he could have lost her.

*You've already lost her, Rafe. Accept it. And move on.*

*Yeah. Move on,* he thought dourly. He'd already tossed a list of phone numbers of past girlfriends into the trash. He'd thrown himself into his work. And yet, he couldn't move on. Not without Lilly. So what was he going to do about it? He didn't have the answer. But there was one thing that was achingly clear to him. He couldn't continue to exist with this kind of misery eating up his insides.

Two days later, on a Friday morning, Lilly left the Silver Horn with tears in her eyes and even when she reached the hospital to begin her shift, she was still sniffing and struggling to hold back the emotional overload.

"You look horrible, Lilly!" Marcella exclaimed as the two women strolled toward the nurses' station. "What's happened now? Did you have another run-in with that cowboy lothario?"

Lilly sighed. "No. I told Bart goodbye this morning. It was his last day of therapy. Greta made him a special cake for the occasion and some of his family was there to share it with him."

"But not Rafe?"

"No. Orin made a point of saying that Rafe was working out on the range—something about an emergency. But I'd rather think he wasn't there because of me."

"Forget him, Lilly. He was born getting anything he wanted whenever he wanted it. He doesn't understand what it means to pay for anything. Not monetarily or emotionally. How can you expect a man like that to be aware of the needs of a woman?"

Marcella was partially right, Lilly thought. Rafe had been born into a privileged life. But not everything had been handed to him. He was hardly a shirker. In fact, he worked above and beyond what a normal man should be expected to do. He loved his family and the Silver Horn and was dedicated to both. He just wasn't dedicated to Lilly. But that hardly made him a bad man.

"I don't want to start my workday thinking of Rafe," she muttered.

"Hmm. Well, Doctor Sherman is on duty today," Marcella said with a smirk. "That will give us both something to think about. We'd better be on our toes."

As the afternoon progressed, Lilly was actually glad the demanding doctor was on duty. His presence helped her to forget that she'd no longer be driving to the Silver Horn every morning to see Bart. Her time with the older man had become more than a physical-therapy job to Lilly and she was going to deeply miss her visits with the ranch patriarch. Almost as much as she missed Rafe.

Rafe. Dear God, ever since that last collision they'd had on the staircase, she'd been replaying their whole relationship over and over in her mind. He'd made her feel alive again. He'd made each day have more meaning. She'd begun to hope and dream and believe in herself as a woman. That was more than any man had ever given her. Had she been wrong in wanting more? True, he'd sworn that his ideas on love and marriage would never change. But maybe if she'd not rushed things and remained at his side, she could have showed him what commitment and loyalty could bring to his life. Eventually, he might have had a change of heart. Instead, she'd given him an ultimatum and pushed him away.

Shaking away that depressing thought, she entered a cubicle where a young woman was being treated for dehydration and heat exhaustion.

"So how's the patient feeling now?" Lilly asked Marcella, who was sponging the frail, redheaded woman with cool water.

"She's improving," Marcella answered, then added in motherly fashion, "And she's learned a lesson not to go on a three-mile jog in the middle of the afternoon."

Lilly was about to give the young woman a word of assurance, when the sound of an approaching siren had her glancing around. The arrival of an ambulance could mean anything from an insect sting to a heart attack. Lilly had learned that each case had to be dealt with cool professionalism. Which was difficult to do when a patient's life was teetering on the edge.

"I'll go see what the ambulance is bringing in," she told Marcella.

She left the cubicle and was heading toward the entryway of the examining rooms, when a gurney being pushed by two medics burst through the double doors.

"What do we have here?"

The question came from Doctor Sherman, who'd suddenly appeared from a doorway to Lilly's left.

"ATV accident. Male. Thirty. Appears to have compound fractures and possible internal injuries," one of the medics answered, then quickly recited the last vital numbers they'd taken on the patient. "This looks like a bad one. He and his buddies were back in the mountains. It took them two hours to get him to a road where the ambulance could pick him up."

"Put him in the first cubicle," the doctor ordered, then wordlessly motioned for Lilly to follow.

For the next five minutes, they worked feverishly to stabilize the man's condition, but just when they thought he could be elevated up to the ICU floor, his blood pressure flattened to nothing and his heart stopped.

Doctor Sherman worked for thirty minutes or more in an effort to regain a heart rhythm, but the injuries were too extensive. Eventually, he looked over at Lilly and shook his head.

"I'm afraid it's over for this young man. I tried. I really tried. What a waste."

The bleak look in the doctor's eyes took Lilly by surprise. It was the first time she'd ever seen the man show any sort of compassion, and she realized that losing this patient had crushed him. But it had crushed Lilly, also. All the while they'd worked over the victim, she couldn't help but compare him to Rafe. The accident victim had been the same age as Rafe and possessed the same robust appearance of a man who worked and played outdoors. Now his life was suddenly over.

"You did everything you could possibly do," she told Doctor Sherman. "You can't feel responsible."

"That doesn't make it any easier when I have to tell his loved ones that he's gone," he said, then walked out of the cubicle.

Miles away, on the Silver Horn, Rafe was standing with Roscoe beneath the flimsy shade of a mesquite tree, letting the horse take a breather, when the clank of a horseshoe against rock sounded behind him.

Expecting it to be one of the ranch hands returning to check on him, he was more than surprised to see his father riding up on his favorite black horse he called Woody. Just seeing Orin back in the saddle perked Rafe's otherwise flat spirits.

Reining his mount to a stop a few steps away from Rafe, Orin climbed down from the saddle.

Rafe greeted him. "Hello, Dad. I see you made it back from Ely okay. I missed you at breakfast this morning. We left early to move these mama cows here to Antelope Creek."

"Clancy told me where you'd be. And I met the crew on their way back to the ranch a few minutes ago. They told me you were still out here," Orin explained as he gazed out toward the small herd of cattle grazing at tufts of buffalo grass along the creek bank. "Looks like the creek is nearly dried up. Is the tank working on this range?"

Any other time Orin's question would've irked Rafe. Making sure that the cattle were always provided with enough fresh water was something he'd learned before he was ten years old. But this time Rafe didn't mind the rudimentary question. His father had ridden at least six miles from the ranch to join him out here. That meant much to Rafe.

"It's full. We checked it yesterday." His gaze took in his father's boots and spurs and the broad, brimmed cowboy hat angled over one eye. Something had finally pushed Orin Calhoun out among the living again and even though Rafe didn't know what it was, he thanked God for it. "What about the cattle in Ely? Are we getting them?"

"They were lightweight, but I bought them at a decent price. If the coming winter isn't too tough, we should be able to add at least a hundred to two hundred more pounds on them. That ought to make a nice profit—if we decide to turn them."

While Roscoe tried to nibble a bean hanging from a branch of the mesquite, Rafe scuffed the toe of his boot against the hard ground. "In case you're wondering, I've apologized to the men. We all have a better understanding now. So there won't be any more problems with me or them."

"That's all I need to know." He stepped over to Woody and began to unbuckle one side of the saddlebags. "I brought a thermos of coffee with me. Want a cup?"

"Sure. Got anything stronger to go in it?" Rafe never had been much for alcohol, but these past few days the momentary relief of a stiff drink was mighty tempting.

Glancing over his shoulder, Orin shot a disapproving glance at his son. "Out here? Hell, you think I'm that much like Dad? He used to carry it in a coffee thermos thinking he could fool me. It's a wonder he hadn't fallen off his horse and broken his fool neck."

"Thank God he doesn't do that anymore," Rafe said.

"Yeah. But he still keeps a bottle of bourbon hidden in his desk."

"Gramps! He's not supposed to be drinking!"

Returning to Rafe's side, Orin handed him a small tin granite cup. He filled it from a metal thermos then fetched another cup for himself. Once they were both sipping the hot drink, Orin said, "As far as I know he's not drinking again. He tells me he keeps a bottle in his desk as a reminder to the mistakes he's made and not to make them again. But after this morning, I'm afraid he might actually dig the thing out."

"Why? What happened this morning? Did he take a bad fall?"

Orin grunted. "Fall? The man can practically dance a jig now. Instead, he's staring out the window, feeling sorry for himself."

"Why? He's one lucky guy. Somebody ought to remind him of that."

Orin thoughtfully stroked his chin with his thumb and forefinger. "He's grieving. Today was his last therapy session with Lilly. Greta made cake and punch for the occasion and we all tried to celebrate. That's why I was late riding out here."

He didn't have to ask if Lilly was there. No doubt she'd been right there at Bart's side. She had the older man's devotion and she loved him for it. Perhaps if Rafe had shown her a bit more devotion, he wouldn't be feeling like a lost little doggie right now. "I wonder why someone didn't let me in on this celebration?" Rafe asked with sarcasm. "What am I around here, some sort of outcast?"

"I didn't know about it myself until Greta told me this morning at breakfast. You were already gone with the men. Besides, I didn't think you'd want to be there. Not with the way things turned out with you and Lilly. Anyway, your brothers didn't know about it until the last minute. And Evan wasn't there, either."

Had Lilly even noticed Rafe's absence? he wondered miserably. Or had she already succeeded in putting him far behind her?

"Lilly or not, I would've been there," Rafe told him. "I love Gramps. I want him to be healthy and to know how proud I am of him."

"Well, I can tell you he's not one bit happy about his time with Lilly ending. He's grown very fond of her, you know."

"Fond! I think he's in love with her!" Rafe muttered.

Orin grunted. "I think you have a much more serious rival for Lilly's affection than Bart."

Rafe choked down the swig of coffee he'd just taken. A rival? The idea that some other man could step into Lilly's life had crossed his mind many times before, but he'd not expected it to be happening now, so soon!

*Go find the nearest mirror and tell the guy looking back at you that he's not quite the Romeo he thinks he is.*

Some of the first words Lilly had spoken to him were coming back to haunt him now, Rafe thought. He wasn't the only man on the planet and she was free to move on to any one of them. He'd given her that choice when he'd walked away from her.

"What are you talking about?" Rafe asked guardedly.

"I'm talking about Chet Anderson."

Rafe wished he could appear indifferent but he couldn't. It was all he could do to keep from leaping onto Roscoe's back and spurring the horse to a mind-clearing gallop across the river flats.

Lifting his hat from his head, he wiped at the sweat that was gluing strands of dark hair to his forehead. "Am I supposed to know who that is?"

"He's the director of nursing at Tahoe General. I think I told you before that he was a friend of mine. He's the one who recommended Lilly to be Bart's therapist."

So in a roundabout way, the man was responsible for Rafe's misery. Chet Anderson had sent Lilly to the Silver Horn, where she'd promptly walked into Rafe's life, turned it upside down, then walked back out. Now Rafe was stumbling around like an idiot who'd lost his bearings.

He jerked his hat down over his forehead. "I can't remember everything you tell me, Dad. I do have a lot on my mind."

Orin continued to sip his coffee. "Well, if you care anything about Lilly, you'd better think about this. Chet is serious about the woman. If he had it his way, he'd marry her tomorrow."

These past three weeks since their breakup, Rafe had wanted to think that Lilly had been just as miserable as he'd been. That she'd been pining to be in his arms and regretting her decision to end their relationship. Dear God, it sounded as though he'd been wrong about that. Along with plenty of other things.

Rafe could feel the blood draining from his face, and the swimmy feeling in the pit of his stomach had him taking long, deep breaths. "How could you know something like that?" he finally asked.

"Chet told me so. Since Lilly has been coming to the ranch for the past two months, he knows that I've gotten acquainted with her and naturally her name has come up in our conversations about Bart. I never had the heart to tell him that you were dating her. Considering your track record with women I figured you'd step out of the way pretty soon, anyway. And you have, haven't you?"

If the two of them had been having this discussion in Orin's office, Rafe could've walked out and not felt too guilty about it. But being out on the open range was different. Sure, he could climb on Roscoe and ride off. But it would leave him looking cowardly and small. Especially after his father had ridden all the way out here to see him. No, whatever his father had to say, Rafe was going to have to brace himself and take it like a man.

"Look, Dad, that's the way Lilly wanted things. I didn't end it, she did!"

Long moments passed before Orin finally asked, "And why was that? Another woman?"

Something in Rafe's throat was closing off, making it difficult for him to breathe, much less talk. Why was his father digging at him like this, tearing away the scab on his wounded heart? "Isn't that my own personal business?" he countered.

"You're right," Orin calmly agreed. "And you don't have to answer. But if you can't talk to me about this, then you're in worse shape than I first imagined."

Rafe directed his gaze to a spot beyond the river to where a ridge of bald mountains rose up from the desert floor. Between here and there, the stout southwesterly wind was whipping up the dry earth and turning the air to a brown haze. His mind was just as foggy as the dusty horizon, he thought dismally, and it was going to take more than a strong wind to clear it.

"There is no other woman, Dad. To be honest, ever

since I met Lilly I've not even wanted to look at any other woman. Our problem is—was—she wants things that I don't. Like love and marriage and kids. That's what tore us apart."

Orin tossed the dregs of his coffee toward a patch of prickly pear. "I figured as much," he said ruefully.

The disappointment on his father's face made Rafe feel even worse. "You don't understand, Dad. Lilly and I had a deal. We weren't supposed to get serious."

Orin shot him a pointed look. "And did you keep your part of the bargain? I don't think so. If you were being honest with me, and yourself, you'd admit that you love Lilly."

*Love!* The word struck him so hard that he unwittingly reached out to brace a hand against Roscoe's strong shoulder. "I don't want to love Lilly. I can't. If I let myself love her…something bad will happen. That's the way things always go, isn't it? That's the way it went for you."

Orin swung his head back and forth. "If you think that, Rafe, you're being a fool."

Rafe walked to the edge of the shade and wiped a cleansing hand over his face. "Dad, how can you, of all people, say that? You lost Darci and then Mom and—"

Orin walked up behind him and laid a hand on his shoulder. "That's exactly why you should be grabbing Lilly and hanging on for all you're worth."

"But Dad, look what losing them has done to you—to all of us!"

Dropping his hand from Rafe's shoulder, Orin moved a few steps away and with his hands resting on his hips, stared out at the river and the grazing cattle. "Whoever told you that life was going to be perfect? Hell, yes, losing my daughter was an agony I can't begin to describe. And when Claudia died, I was completely ripped apart."

Rafe turned toward his father. "Was? You've been ripped apart for years and behaving like you're ninety-two instead of sixty-two! I don't want that happening to me!"

His eyes narrowed against the bright sun, Orin continued to stare out at the red cattle and nearly dry creek bed. "You're right, son. I've not handled a lot of things well—especially when it comes to your mother. Back when Darci died and the two of us were eaten up with grief, she shut me out of her life. At the time I thought I could find relief in another woman. But that was a huge mistake, Rafe. Once you find that special one, any other woman won't do."

Rafe had already come to that conclusion, yet it was a relief to hear his father had reached the same deduction.

"I'm finding that out," Rafe admitted.

Orin sighed. "Cheating on your mother is something I'll carry to my grave. I can't erase the hurt it's caused you boys. But I can try to guide you away from making a mistake and losing the woman you love."

Years of regret were etched upon Orin's face and the sight of it had Rafe momentarily forgetting his own misery. He laid a comforting hand on his father's shoulder. "We forgave you, Dad. And my brothers and I all love having our sister, Sassy, in the family."

Orin gave him a wry smile. "This past year with Sassy coming into my life, Dad having the stroke and now you getting involved with Lilly—all of it opened my eyes to how I've been wasting my life. And that would've made your mother very angry with me. And I'll tell you something else, Rafe. Right about now she'd be very disappointed in you for not stepping up to the plate and marrying Lilly. She would've loved having Lilly in the family, too. We all would."

He certainly couldn't argue that point, Rafe thought. His mother had wished for all her sons to marry and give her grandchildren. Now, the fact that his mother had been friends with Lilly made it seem as though she was speaking to him from the grave, urging him to follow his heart.

The thickness in Rafe's throat was growing steadily worse, making it impossible for him to say a word, and thankfully, his father didn't seem to expect him to.

Finally, he managed to mutter, "I've been behaving like a real bastard, Dad. I don't know why you're even bothering with me."

Orin smiled wanly. "Of all my sons you are more like me than any of the others. You are the spirit of this ranch, Rafe. And I want you to be happy."

Of all the things his father had ever said to him, this had to be the most surprising and by far the most rewarding. And suddenly, everything his father had been saying to him was settling in his mind and filling him with hope.

He said, "I do love Lilly. But each time I think of making a real family with her I get the cold shakes. I'm not as strong as you, Dad. If I lost Lilly—"

"It's not about losing, son," Orin swiftly interrupted. "It's all about loving and living. For as long as you can."

Realizing he was still gripping the empty tin cup, Rafe tossed it to his father. "Are you ready to make the ride back to the ranch? I think it's time I take care of some business in town."

Smiling broadly, Orin patted his son's back. "Let's mount up."

Moments later, the two men were loping side by side, their horses pointed directly toward home.

## Chapter Twelve

Throughout the evening Lilly had done her best to push past their failure to save the accident victim and focus on the stream of ill and injured people that continued to pass through the emergency unit. Even so, the shift had been a taxing one. By the time it ended and Lilly made her way to the locker room, she was utterly drained.

"You look like you're about to fall over," Marcella commented as the two women changed out of their uniforms and into street clothes. "Why don't you come home with me? We'll pick up Harry from Mom's and then all go out to get a burger or pizza."

Lilly pulled a black knit top over her head, then smoothed it into place. "It's nice of you to ask, Marcella, but I couldn't eat a bite. After a day like today I just need a good night's rest."

"Don't we all. I've never seen Doctor Sherman looking so distraught. I almost felt sorry for the man." She tossed a sheepish look over at Lilly. "A few minutes ago, I took him a cup of coffee."

"You did? I'm glad. What did he say?"

"Nothing. Just thanked me. But I didn't do it to gain his favor. I thought it might perk him up a bit." Marcella stepped into a pair of sandals. "Some doctors feel too much, you know? I think he's one of them. In five years' time he'll probably be burned out and dealing used cars somewhere."

Lilly cast her friend a pointed look. "Some nurses feel too much, too. I think I'm looking at her."

Marcella shot her a guilty smile. "Well, something about Peter got to me."

"Something about that accident victim got to me," Lilly admitted. "He reminded me of Rafe in so many ways. Young, strong and clearly adventurous. I've spent all evening imagining how I would feel if an accident took his life."

Frowning, Marcella said, "You'd be devastated, of course. My Lord, Lilly, we're human and we're also nurses. We don't want to see anything happen to even our worst enemies."

But Rafe wasn't her enemy, Lilly thought. He was the man she'd fallen in love with. The man that she still loved and probably always would. Each day that passed without him in her life was a waste. But what could she do about it? She'd cut her ties with him. It was doubtful he'd want to start over. Not after the things she'd said to him and the way they'd parted.

"I'm out of here," Marcella suddenly announced. "See you tomorrow."

Marcella's departure jarred Lilly out of her gloomy thoughts. She waved to her friend as the other woman left the locker room, then turned back to the task of gathering her things. She was stuffing her uniform and shoes into a tote bag when the cell phone in her purse began to jangle.

Since their heated split that night at Lilly's house, Rafe hadn't called her even once. Not that she'd expected him to. Still, that hadn't stopped her from foolishly hoping each time the phone rang.

This time was no different as she fished the device from her purse, but hope quickly vanished the moment she spotted the familiar number. She was hardly in the mood for her mother's rants, but she decided to answer it, anyway. If not, Faye would just keep ringing. And maybe for once, she'd get lucky and her mother would be in an amiable mood.

Clearing her voice, Lilly tried to hide her weariness. "Hi, Mom."

"If you're still at work, I'm sorry, honey," Faye said briskly. "But I just thought I ought to call and let you know what's going on with your parents."

Nothing like getting directly to the point, Lilly thought. With a silent groan, she asked, "What is going on? Have one of you been sick or hurt?"

Her mother chuckled smugly. "No! I'm feeling better than I have in years! I went to see a lawyer today. I've decided to divorce your father."

Years of fighting, squabbling, moaning and yelling had gone on between her parents, but throughout that time Lilly had never heard either one of them ever speak the word *divorce*. Hearing it now, of all days, was too much for Lilly.

"I don't want to hear this, Mother. Not tonight. I think you'd better think this through calmly and after you do, we'll talk about it."

Faye sputtered. "What do you mean you don't want to hear it? You've got to hear it at some point. Later isn't going to make it any easier for you to accept."

Furious over her mother's lack of sensitivity, Lilly muttered, "You know, Mother, I'm beginning to think that's just what you deserve. A good divorcing!"

The woman gasped. "What?"

"You heard me, all right."

"Why would you say such a thing to me?" Faye demanded. "I've been a wonderful mother to you. A dedicated wife to your father. And what have I gotten for it in return? Ron fights me at every turn and you always take his side! Why can't either of you see things my way?"

Except for the *divorce* word, Faye's remarks were nothing new. Lilly had heard it all before. But tonight it was like she was *really* hearing the meaning behind them, and as she stared around the small locker room it felt as though an extra light had switched on and she was seeing everything with stark clarity. For years her mother had tried to force her father to be someone other than himself. Lilly couldn't follow in her mother's footsteps and demand that Rafe be something different. If she ever expected him to want a wife and family, she'd have to show him how wonderful love could be for a lifetime and then allow him to make up his own mind.

"I'll tell you why, Mother. Because not once in your life have you ever considered your husband's wishes. Not once in your life have you ever put him first. If you want to do the right thing you'll stop fighting the man and start loving him, really loving him—before it's too late for either of you!"

Faye sucked in a sharp breath. "Too late! What do you

mean too late? I've been patient. I've given him years to change his ways!"

Sighing, Lilly gentled her voice to an encouraging plea. "Think about it. Just imagine your life without your husband in it. Then maybe you'll understand."

"But, Lilly—"

"Sorry, Mother. I've got to go now. We'll talk later. When we've both calmed down." She lowered the phone from her ear and punched the end button.

Grateful that she had the tiny locker room to herself, Lilly sank onto the dressing bench and covered her face with both hands.

In all her life, she couldn't ever recall feeling as battle weary as she did at this moment. After everything she'd gone through in emergency today, her mother's petty whining seemed ridiculous. And so did her break with Rafe. Being with the man that she loved was more important, more precious than anything. So what if he didn't want to marry her right now? That didn't mean he would always be dead set against making her his wife. As long as they were together, there was always hope that he'd grow into the idea of love and marriage and children. She had to believe that. She had to keep fighting for those things she wanted most.

With sudden decision, Lilly quickly jumped to her feet and grabbed her bag and purse. The hour was already growing late, but she didn't care. She was going to drive out to the Silver Horn and talk with Rafe face-to-face. Even if she had to drag him out of bed to do it.

Moments later, she was striding through the emergency waiting room on her way toward the exit to the parking lot when she spotted Rafe coming through a pair of double glass doors. He caught sight of her immediately and as he walked straight toward her, she couldn't miss the huge bouquet of fresh-cut flowers resting in the crook of one arm. Yet it was the humble, yearning look on his face that really snared her attention and sent her heart into a wild, hopeful flutter.

What was he doing here? After nearly three weeks of ignoring her, why had he suddenly appeared on a night when her heart was weeping for him?

The questions were spinning in her head as she stopped in her tracks and waited for him to reach her side.

Once he was standing in front of her, she asked, "Are you here to visit someone in the hospital? Or are you here to see me?"

A rueful smile twisted his lips. "What do you think?"

As her gaze slowly moved over his rugged features, a sense of sweet familiarity settled in her heart. "You probably won't believe this, but I was planning to drive out to the Silver Horn as soon as I left the building."

Surprise widened his eyes. "To see me? Or Bart?"

There was no sarcasm in his voice and it was suddenly plain to Lilly that a change had taken place in him. But when or why it had come about, she could only wonder.

"I had to tell Bart goodbye this morning," she explained. "It very nearly killed me."

"Because you love him—like a grandfather," he added with a gentle smile.

In spite of the waiting area being full of people, Lilly wanted to step forward and wrap her arms around him. She wanted to hold on to him and never let go. "So you've figured that out?"

His expression turned solemn. "That and a whole lot more."

He offered her the flowers, an armload of red roses,

white daisies and pink carnations. Lilly accepted them and as she hugged them to her breasts, tears began to roll down her cheeks.

"Lilly, we need to talk," he said softly. "Is there somewhere quiet around here?"

Nodding, she placed a hand on his arm and urged him toward a wide wooden door that led into one of the hospital's many chapels.

Inside the quiet sanctuary, the two of them took a seat together on one of the back pews. As soon as they were settled, Rafe used his finger to wipe the tears from her cheeks.

"Lilly, were you really planning to drive to the ranch to see me?"

He reached for both her hands and as his fingers folded tightly around hers, she realized that no matter how he felt about her, she would love him for the rest of her life.

Her eyes still wet with tears, she nodded. "Today I— well, I won't go into everything that's happened, but I'll just say that my eyes are open now, Rafe. I love you. If that's something—"

Before she could get the rest of the words out, he pulled her tightly against him. With his face buried in the silky curtain of her hair, he groaned with anguish. "Oh, Lilly, I thought I'd lost you and I didn't know how I was going to go on."

Tilting her head back, she gazed up at his anguished face. "I was expecting too much of you too soon, Rafe. I'm sorry that I didn't understand that before now."

"No, Lilly. I'm the one who should be down on my knees begging you for forgiveness," he whispered ruefully. "You deserved so much more than I was willing to give you."

Cradling his face with her palms, she said, "And you deserved a little more understanding from me. Tonight I was sickened to think that I've been behaving like my mother—demanding and thinking only about what I want rather than what you want and need. Can you forgive me for that, Rafe?"

His gray eyes were suddenly lit with a light so soft and gentle it nearly took her breath away.

"Oh, Lilly. Love. Marriage. Children. Instead of embracing the idea of having a family, the thought of those things always sent a chill right through me. My dad lost a child and then his wife. I watched him grieve and change into a man I hardly knew. I watched our happy home turn into a dark place. And I swore that I'd never set up my heart to that sort of risk. From then on I jumped from one woman to the next, not giving myself a chance to care about any of them. Until I met you and suddenly I didn't want to jump anymore. I tried not to think of you as my wife. I tried to tell myself I wouldn't want you to have my babies. But deep down I knew I was fooling myself. And I hated myself for not having the courage to admit it to myself and to you."

"Everything about life is a risk, Rafe. Especially if you want to live it to the fullest."

"Lilly, my darling," he whispered hoarsely. "I couldn't see exactly what you meant to me until my father pried my eyes open. And I can tell you right now, it scared the hell out of me when it finally dawned on me exactly how much I love you."

Joy and disbelief swept through her. "Love? Did I hear you right?"

His lips twisted to a wry slant. "Bet you never expected to hear that from me."

"No. But down deep I never quit hoping. That's what I was planning on telling you tonight. That no matter how long it took I wasn't going to give up on you."

He gently stroked a hand through her hair. "Such a patient woman," he murmured. "I just hope you can put up with me for the rest of our lives."

Still unsure of this new Rafe she was seeing, her misty gaze searched his face. "The rest of our lives? What about all those strings you were worried about?"

He brought his lips close to hers. "Rope me. Tie me. Marry me. That's all I want."

"Is that a proposal?"

To answer, he kissed her thoroughly, then pulled a small, velvet box from his shirt pocket.

"I picked this out in a hurry," he admitted, as he flipped open the lid. "So if you'd rather have something else, you can change it."

Her head reeling with indescribable joy, she stared at the large diamond encircled by smaller stones and a plain narrow band nestled beneath the engagement ring.

Laughter bubbled from her as she wound her arms around his neck and kissed him soundly. Then finally she eased her head back and looked at him with all the love that was bubbling in her heart. "I wouldn't change it or you for anything. But I would like to know what kind of magic your father worked on you."

A clever smile touched his lips. "Let's just say he made me see that I didn't want you to be anybody's wife but mine."

He took the ring from its case and slipped it onto her finger. "So you want to tell me what happened to turn your thinking around?"

Her eyes full of love, she cradled her palm against his

cheek. "Let's just say I suddenly understood how very, very precious you are to me."

He slanted her a grin. "So you think you can put up with a dusty cowboy who puts too many long hours in the saddle?"

"I can. Do you think you can put up with a nurse who cares too much for her patients?"

"The fact that you're a nurse who cares too much only makes me love you more, Lilly. And I promise I'll never let my job get in the way of our love."

She pressed a kiss upon his cheek. "And I'll never let my job come before you or our children, my darling."

His expression turned serious. "Do you think you'll like living in the ranch house?" he asked. "You might not want to be stuck in a house full of men. If you want I can build another house. We—"

She stopped his words with a gentle finger to his lips. "Rafe, I wouldn't want to live anywhere but in the ranch house. I've always wanted to be surrounded by a big, loving family. And being near Bart will be a special treat. We're going to be happy," she promised. "Together. For the rest of our lives."

He looked at her for long, tender moments then suddenly jumped to his feet. "Come on," he urged as he tugged her up from the wooden bench. "Let's go to the ranch and tell everybody we're getting married!"

"It's getting late, Rafe! Everyone will be in bed!" she exclaimed as he hustled her out of the chapel.

"Then we'll get them out of bed. I can't wait to see the look on Dad's face when he hears the news."

Smiling broadly, she admitted, "Well, I would like to see Bart's reaction."

Rafe chuckled. "He's going to be jealous."

"No, he's going to be happy," she told him. "And so will we—be happy—for the rest of our lives."

They stepped through a pair of glass doors and onto the sidewalk. The clear night sky was twinkling with stars and as Lilly looked in the direction of the Silver Horn, she wrapped her arm around Rafe's. Their love, their life together was only beginning and the future couldn't look more beautiful than it did at this moment.

## *Epilogue*

"Look at her face. If she had wings she'd look just like a little cherub."

The comment came from Finn as he peered into the ruffled bassinet at his six-week-old niece, Colleen Claudia Calhoun. Rafe and Lilly's daughter had been christened earlier that morning at Our Lady of Sierra, the same church where they had wed only a little more than eleven months ago.

Throughout most of the afternoon, the Silver Spur ranch house had been full of friends and relatives who'd shown up to celebrate the happy occasion. But the long, August day was coming to a close and most of the visitors had departed. Now Colleen, as everyone called the baby girl, was getting the full focus of attention from her doting family.

Standing on the opposite side of the bassinet, Rafe had Lilly hugged close to his side as they all gazed down at the wide-awake baby dressed in soft white lace. Her eyes were gray like her father's, while the sparse bit of hair on top of her head was golden-blond like her mother's. For the special event today, Lilly had attached a tiny white bow with a pink rosette to the little curls. Each time Rafe looked at his daughter, his heart brimmed with so much love and pride, he was very nearly overcome with emotion.

"She might look like a cherub," he said to Finn, "but when she's having one of her crying fits she's louder than a braying donkey."

"Rafe!" Lilly laughingly scolded. "Colleen is going to love hearing that her daddy once compared her to a donkey!"

From a nearby easy chair, Clancy teased, "She inherited her loud mouth from you, brother."

"Be glad she's got a loud mouth," Finn said. "That way she won't have any trouble telling the boys to get lost."

"That isn't going to be a problem," Rafe joked. "I'm not going to let her date until she's thirty."

Finn laughed. "Good luck, brother. I expect you'll be letting her drive into town by the time she's sixteen."

"Not in a sports car and only if her mother or father is with her," Rafe assured him.

Finn and Clancy were still laughing at their brother's overly protective plan when Bart walked over and promptly scooped the baby into his arms.

"Quit fussing over her like she's Calhoun property," he scolded his grandsons. "It's time I take her outside and show her what she's going to inherit someday."

As Bart walked away with the baby, Finn looked over at Rafe and rolled his eyes. "Calhoun property? He thinks little Colleen is his."

Rafe and Lilly both laughed. Their daughter's arrival had changed both their lives in so many amazing and wonderful ways. The baby had also twisted a house full of bachelors around her tiny finger. There was a sense of renewed joy in the Silver Horn ranch house now, and Rafe couldn't thank God enough for bringing Lilly into his life.

"We wouldn't want it any other way," Rafe said fondly. "Colleen has given him another purpose besides making money."

"So when can we expect little Colleen to get a baby brother?" Finn asked coyly. "We need another foreman coming up in the ranks."

Lilly released a good-natured groan. "Give us time, Finn."

"That's right," Rafe said pointedly. "A thing like that requires plenty of hard work and losing lots of sleep."

While Finn let out a loud, lusty laugh, a grinning Rafe urged Lilly toward the same door where Bart had exited with the baby.

"Let's go outside and see how our little princess likes surveying her kingdom," he said to his wife.

Outside on the patio, Rafe held Lilly close to his side, while across the way, Bart stood at the yard fence with baby Colleen safely ensconced in the crook of his arm.

"She's quiet," Lilly remarked. "She must be enjoying the stories her great-grandfather is telling her."

Rafe fondly watched on as Bart moved farther down the fence, then paused to point to the big red horse barn where most of the foals were born.

"I'll tell you what he's doing," Rafe said wryly. "He's promising her a pony of her own. Among other things. We're going to have a hell of a time keeping him and Dad from spoiling her rotten."

"Oh, I'm sure we'll manage to keep her grounded enough."

"Looking at him now, it's impossible to tell that Gramps ever suffered such a severe stroke. God blessed him by giving him you for a nurse."

She looked up at him, her brown eyes sparkling with affection. "He also blessed me by bringing me here," she said, then chuckled softly. "I'll be honest. At first I wasn't sure about taking on the role of Bart's therapy nurse. I thought I'd probably be walking into a den of male lions."

He grinned. "And what do you think now?"

Her arm tightened against the back of his waist. "That you're all a bunch of lambs."

"Don't let that get out," he said with a laugh. "You'll ruin the tough Calhoun reputation."

Sighing, she rested her cheek against his arm. "The christening was beautiful. And I'm so glad that Marcella and her two boys came out here to the ranch to help us celebrate this afternoon. I don't get to see her nearly as much now that the two of us are no longer working the emergency unit."

"Well, your lives are changing. Since she adopted Peter, she has two boys to care for. And you have me and Colleen to corral."

"And that's a task I dearly love," she assured him.

"So you're not disappointed about giving up your job at Tahoe General to work part-time at Lakeside Clinic?"

"Not in the least," she said, then straightening away from his arm, she cast him a pointed look. "Today at the church when Father O'Bannon took Colleen in his arms, I looked at you and wondered how you really felt about us having a child so soon after we got married. Maybe I shouldn't have quit my birth control so soon—but I thought it would take a few months before my body would even think about getting pregnant. Instead, it was a few weeks. In fact, I'm pretty sure Colleen was conceived when you took me on that ride to Eagle's Ridge to show me that beautiful spot you'd discovered. Remember?"

His grin was slow and suggestive. "Every minute of it, my sweet wife. Just thinking about it now makes me want to carry you inside to our bedroom. But as for you getting pregnant so quickly—I wouldn't change that at all. You and our daughter mean more to me than anything. And I happen to think Finn has a good idea. I want more babies to go with Colleen. That is, if you're willing to give them to me."

Looping her arm through his, she squeezed it tight. "I couldn't deny you anything, Rafe. But we might consider stopping after four or five more babies. Otherwise, the ranch house might get crowded."

Laughing, Rafe gestured toward his grandfather. "Do you think for a minute that Gramps wouldn't build more rooms? He views his great-grandchildren as the future of the Silver Horn. Sassy and Jett's son and little Colleen have given new meaning to his life."

Her happy gaze lingered on Bart and their daughter. "I think you're right. And I think having a grandchild has even helped my mother learn about loving."

"Hmm. I'm glad your parents were here today. And they seemed happy enough," Rafe commented. "Your mother was right in not going through with the divorce."

"She has a long way to go, but she's trying to be less demanding and more understanding," Lilly admitted.

"Speaking of parents," Rafe said, "I was more than surprised to see that Dad had invited Noreen Moreland to attend the christening with him."

Lilly looked at him with surprise. "I thought she was only a business associate."

"What sort of business would Dad have with the Deputy District Attorney of Carson County? Other than the kind a red-blooded man has with a beautiful woman."

A thoughtful smile crossed Lilly's face. "Actually, now that I think of it, she was very attractive."

"Kind of young for him, though, don't you think?"

Lilly rose up on her toes and kissed his cheek. "Age has nothing to do with love."

Groaning with contentment, he pulled her into the tight circle of his arms and lowered his mouth to hers. "But it has everything to do with us. Thank you, my sweet wife, for teaching me that."

"You were a stubborn student," she whispered against his lips. "But you finally came around."

"Yeah. And I'm going to stay around." He eased his head back to give her a naughty grin. "By the way, did I tell you that I ran across another beautiful spot on the ranch that I want to show you?"

Happy laughter tinkled out of Lilly, and across the yard Bart smiled smugly at the baby in his arms.

\* \* \* \* \*

*One Calhoun man down and more to go!
Don't miss the next* MEN OF THE WEST
*when Clancy finds his match!*

# COMING NEXT MONTH FROM

**H** HARLEQUIN®

# SPECIAL EDITION

## Available August 19, 2014

### #2353 MAVERICK FOR HIRE
*Montana Mavericks: 20 Years in the Saddle!* • by Leanne Banks
Nick Pritchett has a love 'em and leave 'em attitude...except when it comes to his best friend, Cecelia Clifton. When the pretty brunette insists on finding a beau, the hunky carpenter realizes that he can't lose Cecelia to another man. Nick may be Mr. Fix-It in Rust Creek Falls, but his BFF has done a number on his heart!

### #2354 WEARING THE RANCHER'S RING
*Men of the West* • by Stella Bagwell
Cowboy Clancy Calhoun always had room for only one woman in his heart—his ex-fiancée, Olivia Parsons, who left him years ago. So when Olivia returns home to Nevada for work, Clancy is blown away. But can the handsome rancher simultaneously heal his wounded heart *and* convince Olivia to start a life together at long last?

### #2355 A MATCH MADE BY BABY
*The Mommy Club* • by Karen Rose Smith
Adam Preston never worried about babies...that is, until he had his sister's infant to care for! Bewildered at his new responsibilities, Adam asks pediatrician Kaitlyn Foster for help. The good doctor is reluctant to give her assistance, but once she does, she just can't resist the bachelor and his adorable niece.

### #2356 NOT JUST A COWBOY
*Texas Rescue* • by Caro Carson
Texan oil heiress Patricia Cargill is particular when it comes to her men, but there's just something about Luke Waterson she can't resist. Maybe it's that he's a drop-dead gorgeous rescue fireman and ranch hand! Luke, who lights long-dormant fires in Patricia, has also got his fair share of secrets. Can the cowboy charm the socialite into a happily-ever-after?

### #2357 ONCE UPON A BRIDE
by Helen Lacey
Although she owns a bridal shop, Lauren Jakowski can't imagine herself taking the trip down the aisle anytime soon. In fact, she's sworn off men for the foreseeable future! But Cupid intervenes in the form of her new next-door neighbor, Gabe Vitali. Despite his tragic past, the cancer survivor might just be the key to Lauren's future.

### #2358 HIS TEXAS FOREVER FAMILY
by Amy Woods
After a difficult divorce, art teacher Liam Campbell wants nothing more than to start anew in Peach Leaf, Texas. He's instantly captivated by his new boss, Paige Graham, but the lovely widow has placed romance on the back burner to care for her emotionally wounded young son and focus on her career. Still, as Liam bonds with the boy and his mother, a new family begins to blossom.

---

**YOU CAN FIND MORE INFORMATION ON UPCOMING HARLEQUIN® TITLES, FREE EXCERPTS AND MORE AT WWW.HARLEQUIN.COM.**

HSECNM0814

# REQUEST YOUR FREE BOOKS!

## 2 FREE NOVELS PLUS 2 FREE GIFTS!

### ⊕ HARLEQUIN®

# SPECIAL EDITION

## Life, Love & Family

---

**YES!** Please send me 2 FREE Harlequin® Special Edition novels and my 2 FREE gifts (gifts are worth about $10). After receiving them, if I don't wish to receive any more books, I can return the shipping statement marked "cancel." If I don't cancel, I will receive 6 brand-new novels every month and be billed just $4.74 per book in the U.S. or $5.24 per book in Canada. That's a savings of at least 14% off the cover price! It's quite a bargain! Shipping and handling is just 50¢ per book in the U.S. and 75¢ per book in Canada.* I understand that accepting the 2 free books and gifts places me under no obligation to buy anything. I can always return a shipment and cancel at any time. Even if I never buy another book, the two free books and gifts are mine to keep forever.

235/335 HDN F45Y

| Name | (PLEASE PRINT) | |
|------|------|------|

| Address | | Apt. # |
|------|------|------|

| City | State/Prov. | Zip/Postal Code |
|------|------|------|

Signature (if under 18, a parent or guardian must sign)

Mail to the **Harlequin® Reader Service:**
**IN U.S.A.:** P.O. Box 1867, Buffalo, NY 14240-1867
**IN CANADA:** P.O. Box 609, Fort Erie, Ontario L2A 5X3

**Want to try two free books from another line?**
**Call 1-800-873-8635 or visit www.ReaderService.com.**

* Terms and prices subject to change without notice. Prices do not include applicable taxes. Sales tax applicable in N.Y. Canadian residents will be charged applicable taxes. Offer not valid in Quebec. This offer is limited to one order per household. Not valid for current subscribers to Harlequin Special Edition books. All orders subject to credit approval. Credit or debit balances in a customer's account(s) may be offset by any other outstanding balance owed by or to the customer. Please allow 4 to 6 weeks for delivery. Offer available while quantities last.

**Your Privacy**—The Harlequin® Reader Service is committed to protecting your privacy. Our Privacy Policy is available online at www.ReaderService.com or upon request from the Harlequin Reader Service.

We make a portion of our mailing list available to reputable third parties that offer products we believe may interest you. If you prefer that we not exchange your name with third parties, or if you wish to clarify or modify your communication preferences, please visit us at www.ReaderService.com/consumerchoice or write to us at Harlequin Reader Service Preference Service, P.O. Box 9062, Buffalo, NY 14269. Include your complete name and address.

---

HSE13R

SPECIAL EXCERPT FROM

**H** HARLEQUIN®

## SPECIAL EDITION

*Cecelia Clifton came to Rust Creek Falls hoping to find true love. Then she fell for Nick Pritchett, the commitment-phobic Thunder Canyon carpenter she's known all her life. But when Nick agrees to give his best friend boyfriend-catching lessons, he discovers that there's more to Cecelia than meets the eye—and that he wants her all for himself!*

\*\*\*

"I know these are for the charity auction, but if I give you twenty-five bucks, will you give me a bite of something?"

He must be desperate, Cecelia thought. Plus there was also the fact that she knew that Nick did a lot of charity work. He was always helping out people who couldn't pay him. Her heart softened a teensy bit. "Okay. Two apple muffins for twenty-five bucks. Frosting or not?"

"I'll take one naked," he said and shot her a naughty look. "The other frosted."

His sexy expression got under her skin, but she told herself to ignore it. She handed him a hot cupcake. "It's hot," she warned, but he'd already stuffed it into his mouth.

He opened his mouth and took short breaths.

She shook her head. "When will you learn? When?" she asked and frosted a cupcake, then set it in front of him. "Now that you've singed your taste buds," she said.

He walked to the fridge and grabbed a beer then gulped it down. "Now for the second," he said.

"Where's my twenty-five bucks?" she asked.

"You know I'm good for it," he said and pulled out his wallet. He extracted the cash and gave it to her. "There."

"Thank you very much," she said and put the cash in her pocket.

Within two moments, he'd scarfed down the second cupcake, then pulled a sad expression. "Are you sure you can't give me one more?"

"I'm sure," she said.

He sighed. "Hard woman," he said, shaking his head. "Hard, hard woman."

"One of my many charms," she said and smiled. "You always eat the baked goods I give you in two bites. Don't you know how to savor anything?"

He met her gaze for a long moment. His eyes became hooded and he gave her a smile that branded her from her head to her toes. "There's only one way for you to find out."

\*\*\*

*Enjoy this sneak peek from*
*MAVERICK FOR HIRE*
*by* New York Times *bestselling author Leanne Banks,*
*the newest installment in the brand-new six-book continuity*
***MONTANA MAVERICKS:***
***20 YEARS IN THE SADDLE!,***
*coming in September 2014!*

# HARLEQUIN®

# SPECIAL EDITION

**Life, Love and Family**

Coming in September 2014

## *WEARING THE RANCHER'S RING*
by *USA TODAY* bestselling author
# Stella Bagwell

Cowboy Clancy Calhoun always had room for
only one woman in his heart—his ex-fiancée,
Olivia Parsons, who left him six years ago.
So, when Olivia returns home to Nevada for work,
Clancy is blown away. But can the handsome
rancher simultaneously heal his wounded heart *and*
convince Olivia to start a life together, at long last?

**Don't miss the latest edition of the
*MEN OF THE WEST* miniseries!**

*Enjoy **THE BABY TRUTH** and
**ONE TALL, DUSTY COWBOY**,
already available from the
**MEN OF THE WEST** miniseries by Stella Bagwell.*

*Available wherever books and ebooks are sold.*

# Just Can't Get Enough of... Lawmen!

You'll be on the edge of your seat all month long with all the excitement that these fearless lawmen bring.

Starting with...
## *MAVERICK SHERIFF*
by Delores Fossen

Thrown into a dangerous investigation, Sheriff Cooper McKinnon and assistant district attorney Jessa Wells must join forces to protect the baby they each claim as their own.

And don't miss
## *WAY OF THE SHADOWS*
by Cynthia Eden

FBI profiler Noelle Evers can't remember him...but former army ranger Thomas Anthony would kill in order to protect the one woman he can't live without. With Noelle once again in a predator's sights, can Thomas save the woman he loves a second time?

All available September 2014 from

**HARLEQUIN**
™

# INTRIGUE®
EDGE-OF-YOUR-SEAT INTRIGUE,
FEARLESS ROMANCE.

www.Harlequin.com

HIIBC0814

ISBN-13:978-0-373-65831-2

## SPECIAL EDITION

# SADDLE UP FOR THE LOVE OF A LIFETIME

After losing her heart—and her baby—to a disastrous romance, Lilly Lockett has her mind on only one thing: her job. She's come to the Silver Horn Ranch in Nevada to look after the Calhoun family patriarch, nothing more. But when she encounters rakish ranch foreman Rafe Calhoun, it's fireworks at first sight!

Playboy Rafe knows his grandfather's new nurse is all wrong for him. He decided long ago that relationships just aren't in the cards. A few dates, then move on—that's been his motto. But an attempt at a casual affair with Lilly soon becomes all too serious...for both of them. And soon Rafe has to make a choice: to keep flying solo, or risk everything for a future with the woman he's come to love.

$5.50 U.S./$6.25 CAN.

ISBN-13: 978-0-373-65831-2

50550

9 780373 658312

E A N

S

CATEGORY
HOME AND FAMILY

HARLEQUIN®
SPECIAL
EDITION
harlequin.com